In The Shadows

Tara Lyons

Also By Tara Lyons

Have you read the book 2 and 3 in the DI Hamilton series

No Safe Home

Deadly Friendship

For my family – my inspiration.

I dedicate this book to a very special group of friends who set me on my writing journey. Throughout these pages I've used their names as my way of saying thank you.

To my mentor, dear friend and writing partner in crime, Mel Comley; my dream would never have been fulfilled if it were not for her.

Special thanks go to my editor Stefanie Spangler Buswell, cover designer Karri Klawiter and my beta readers Maria Lee and Noelle Holten – your feedback was instrumental. Also, to Linda Prather for her guidance and Joseph Calleja for his proofreading skills and advice – I thank you both dearly.

Lastly, thank you to The Book Club on Facebook, the amazing bloggers and online friends I've made over the last year. The support, encouragement and banter is always a welcome tonic.

PROLOGUE

They never found the first dead body. I didn't want them to. I was in control, powerful, and important. My fingers tightly gripped the smooth black knife handle, and I felt the rush of excitement as the sharp tip pierced her chest. All my energy, power, and hate spurred me on, telling me to push harder—so hard that I saw the last breath escape her dark lips and mingle with the frosty midnight air.

It was the first time I took someone's life, and the rush was euphoric. No drug or liquor could evoke that pleasure; it was better than sex. Even the memory of that night makes my skin tingle. It wasn't planned, and I'd had no real clue what I was doing or what I was even thinking about in the minutes that ultimately led to my greatest moment. She goaded me and forced me into making that decision, which ended her pathetic life. I can't let wrongdoers walk these streets, those selfish, thoughtless, and insignificant people.

But mistakes were made, and I need to learn from them. She'd clawed at my face. My flesh and blood were stained forever under her manicured nails. She took a piece of me with her into the dirt, into her burial ground. I kicked her in the face for that.

I spent time and sweat on her, digging the wet mud. She got more from me than I would have liked. The strain was worth it to know that no one will find her—of that I'm sure.

I watch, sometimes, as people walk over her. Women stupidly totter, workmen stomp, and children kick their footballs right above her lifeless body. None of them will find her because none of them will stop long enough to take in the world around them, to worry about another individual, or to notice who is watching them. She was my rehearsal. They all will be, until I reach my ultimate prize.

No one will ever make me feel the sorrow she did—reduced to tears by her words, like a child in the playground. She didn't listen to me or give me the respect that I deserved; she needed to pay for her actions. My pain has turned to fury, and I won't be stopped. They'll all pay. They won't ignore me. They'll fear me.

I know what I have to do next, and the only thing missing now is opportunity. I need to ensure that I make clever decisions, and for that, I need time to plan. But time is my constant companion right now, which I must manipulate to my advantage. My moment will come. I watch her every move. I listen and linger undetected. I know she'll slip up soon, and that will be my opening to strike and crush her life. I will extinguish her forever. I'll be the one in the spotlight again.

But I can be patient. For now, I'll watch from the shadows.

CHAPTER ONE

The head emerged from the water first. Dangling back, it hung awkwardly. Wet black hair stuck to the scalp, face, and neck. The odd strand slipped into her mouth. Her glassy brown eyes were wide open, frozen in time, as her naked body bobbed in and out of the icy cold water. A film of grit from the River Thames clung to her body and discoloured her white skin with a tinge of dirty brown. Beneath that, her body was flawless, toned and slim with pert breasts the ideal size for her small frame. Freshly french-manicured nails, which were now caked in London's sewerage water, were another sign that she'd taken care of herself. She had no tattoos, scars, or imperfections, except for the gaping wound in her chest.

Detective Inspector Denis Hamilton wrapped his red scarf a little tighter around the neck of his long, tailored, wool coat as he watched the scene from the river bank. He wanted to survey the surrounding area, soak up all the visual information possible before joining the team to gather the specifics. He was clean-shaven, as always, despite the early hour. But he wished he had grabbed his hat before rushing from his home because his cropped hair was useless at shielding the chill. He shoved his hands deep into his coat pockets, sighed heavily, and made his way towards the murder scene.

The police divers struggled to the bank with her lifeless body, where the pathology team was in place and waiting. They had erected a white tent twenty feet from the edge of the river to examine the woman and collect evidence from the water.

"What are you waiting for?" questioned the head pathologist, Laura Joseph. "Bring her body into the tent immediately! The less she's exposed to the elements, the better chance we have to determine exactly what happened here." She urgently ushered the divers into the tent.

Hamilton caught up with his partner, Detective Sergeant Lewis Clarke on the pathway adjacent to the tent. "Nice of you to join us, gov." Clarke greeted him with the usual sarcasm.

"Unlike you, Lewis, I do not enjoy being summoned from my bed at three a.m. on a cold December morning," he replied abruptly. "I would like to spend a few moments in bed with my wife before being called out on the next case."

"Only takes you a few moments, eh?" Clarke continued to jest, but evidently clocked the stern expression on his partner's face. "Sorry, gov, how is the missus?"

"We're not here for chit-chat, Lewis. And to be perfectly honest, I'm not in the mood anyway. Let's head over, and you can brief me on what you know so far."

Hamilton and Clarke had been partners for four years, so they were comfortable with each other's attitudes. The detectives quickly stomped through the crisp leaves, scrunching under their heavy footsteps, and Clarke explained that he didn't have any information about the victim as yet. A forensic pathologist stood by the entrance of the tent and handed them each a pair of shoe covers.

"Don't want you contaminating our scene now do we, detectives?" The man smiled.

"Thanks," Hamilton replied as he slipped the woven disposable material over his shiny black brogues.

When they were both ready, he pulled back the flap of the tent and entered to find Laura bent over the dead body.

"So what can you tell us?" Clarke fired the first question, not bothering with pleasantries.

"Well, she's dead," Laura returned coldly.

"Okay, this is going to get us nowhere." Hamilton sighed. "Good morning, night, or afternoon—however you want to greet each other at ungodly hour, I don't really care. But let's show some degree of professionalism."

The pathologist stood on one side of the tent and glared at the two detectives opposite her. Nobody spoke. The wind howled against the thin white tent surrounding them, the cold weather mirroring the frosty atmosphere.

Hamilton had no choice but to take charge of the situation. "It's freezing. You have your job to do, and we have ours, so can you please tell us what you've discovered so far? Then we can leave you in peace to start your investigation."

Laura rolled her eyes but said nothing. Hamilton knew she didn't have a problem with detectives from the London Metropolitan Police as a whole, but Clarke brought out the worst in her. The pair had shared a rocky past, and he didn't want to encourage a resurgence in the middle of a crime scene. He was confident she would play ball, if only to get his partner out of her tent.

She answered, looking directly at Hamilton. "I don't think this one should be too hard for you, boys." Laura let her words hang in the air for a moment longer than necessary. "The victim's name is Michelle Young. She was twenty-seven years of age and lived right here in Central London. Of course, you'll have to wait until after the post-mortem for the official cause of death, but off the record, she died from a single stab wound to the heart."

CHAPTER TWO

Grace bolted up in bed, panicking. Sweat dripped down her forehead, and her hair stuck to her clammy neck. She panted sharply and tapped the base of her bedside lamp, summoning the light into the room. Her eyes adjusted to her surroundings. The pristine black suit dress and jacket hung on the wardrobe door, fresh from the dry-cleaner's. The walls were covered in photographs of happy, smiling friends and family, and the shelves were crammed with an enormous book collection. She was safe at home. Although her breathing slowly began to steady to an even pace, and the visions of her nightmare had faded to a blur, she couldn't shake the terrifying feeling. That was the first night Grace dreamt of a dead body.

Her heavy eyelids tricked her into believing she had been asleep for only twenty minutes; she was surprised to find it was 6:50 a.m. and had actually been sleeping for hours. Diving back under the duvet was pointless since the alarm was set to go off in ten minutes. Grace needed to shower, get dressed, and mentally prepare herself. She had only two hours until the funeral car arrived. It was the day she had been dreading for three weeks. Grace was a strong, confident, and independent person. But she feared she wouldn't have the strength to cope, because this was the day she had to bury her grandfather.

She absently went through the motions of drying and styling her hair into a neat ponytail; she didn't want the fuss of it falling on her face today. Staring into space, she drew the black opaque tights over her legs and dressed in her smart but grim suit. She had fallen deep into her memories of the man she'd idolised for as long as she could remember. The knocking on her bedroom door was an unwanted wake-up call, so she ignored the noise.

"Darling, the car is downstairs." Valerie, Grace's mother, called from the other side of the door.

Although she offered no reply, Grace heard her mother open the door and walk up behind her. She kept her back turned to Valerie, desperate to stare out the window and stay wrapped in her daydream.

"Sweetheart, the car is downstairs. We're waiting for you."

"I know. I'm coming," Grace replied softly, then finally turned to face her mother.

Neither of them had cried that morning, so they weren't flush-faced or red-eyed. But her own face surely mirrored her mother's pale and drained face, as they were similar in looks as much as personality. Valerie's eyes held a sorrowful gaze that Grace understood deeply, one that no fake smile could hide; so they didn't try to fake it with each other. Instead, they hugged tightly, and Grace tried to take some strength from the embrace. Once they'd let go, they silently walked downstairs together, out the front door and to the funeral car.

After the service and burial at Kensal Green Cemetery, family and friends came together at The Coach and Horses Public House to pay their respects to a well-liked and respected man. The crowd sang old Irish folk songs and plenty of food, and more than one pint of Guinness, was had by many. Grace wasn't prepared for the pleasantries and devastated looks. She abhorred the way people tilted their heads when they enquired about how she was coping. She hated when people asked her that, and wondered if it would go down in history as the worst question to ask at a funeral. She told her family she needed some fresh air and would be back shortly, but instead, she found herself walking back to the cemetery to spend a little extra time at her grandfather's burial place.

"I miss you, Granddad. You were my best friend," Grace sobbed through her words. She spoke to the pile of dirt that had filled the vast hole in the ground that now held her grandfather's coffin. "How will I get through Christmas without you?"

She thought of years gone by, of Christmas mornings spent with her mum and dad rushing through breakfast to meet her grandparents in their local pub for a few festive beverages. The meat would have been cooked the night before, and the potatoes and vegetables put on the boil before everyone headed out into the cold Christmas morning. Her grandfather knew everyone in their local pub, and they would all celebrate together before rambling back for dinner and an early evening snooze.

Now she sat on the wet grass, pained by the realisation of never seeing the most influential man in her life again. The dark clouds rumbled above and warned of the torrent they were preparing to unleash.

"But I don't want to leave you." Grace threw her arms over the dirt, trying to get closer to her grandfather, and bawled. Safe in the knowledge that no one could see her breakdown, she allowed the ground to dampen her clothes while she dampened the soil with her tears in return.

Half an hour later, she sat up and tried to regain some control over her emotions. The first wet droplet smacked down on her head.

"I think that really is my sign to leave. I know you hated these emotional outbursts anyway. My kidneys are too close to my eyes, I suppose." She smiled at the thought of the saying her grandfather used when anyone dared cry in his company.

Grace got to her feet and drew a few deep breaths. She had mustered enough courage to return to her family and mourn with them.

"I definitely need a few drinks," she said, patting the earth a final time before leaving the cemetery.

CHAPTER THREE

The bile rose in Grace's mouth, and with no chance of making it to the bathroom, she hung her body over the side of the bed and threw up over her wooden bedroom floor. The translucent vomit formed a puddle as she pulled herself into an upright position. She reached over to her bedside table and wanted to cry when she realised the glass of water, that she normally took to bed with her every night, wasn't there. The room spun, drummers used the inside of her head as an instrument, and her tongue felt like sandpaper. The sickly feeling took hold of her again, and she jerked to the side once more, unable to control the violent rejection her stomach had to its contents.

She mustered the energy to pull herself up again and was startled to find her mother standing in the doorway. Grace shook her head and held up her hand, fearing an imminent lecture. Valerie stepped into the room, eyeing her with disdain, but Grace was more interested in what she held in her hands: a glass of water and a packet of painkillers. She reached out weakly, and Valerie walked over to her.

"Well, look at the state of you." Her mother's mouth turned down. "You should be ashamed of yourself, Grace Murphy. Getting wasted at your grandfather's wake is one thing, and maybe I could have put it down to grief, but downing shots at the bar and dancing on tables! Then just up and leaving without so much as a goodbye. I'm so disappointed in you. I can't believe you acted like that. Your grandfather would have been ashamed."

Grace felt her mother's voice boom through her delicate ears as if she had used a microphone. She searched her memories but drew a blank. "I'm sorry, Mum. I can't remember anything from the wake." She rubbed her forehead.

"Sleep it off, Grace. I'll clean up this mess."

She obliged, and her mother's words faded into the distance as she lowered her head onto the pillow and allowed her heavy, hungover eyes to close.

****

"What?" A croaky voice grunted down the phone line.

"Lewis, get your arse out of bed. Another body's been found. Meet me at Hyde Park, by the Serpentine. Now!" Hamilton demanded before he ended the call.

Regardless of the fact his wife had grown accustomed to him leaving at all hours in the morning, Hamilton still left a note on the bedside table. He was at the crime scene by four a.m. and waited in his car, out of the early morning chill, until his partner pulled up next to him ten minutes later.

"Let's get moving, Lewis. I want to be out of here before dog walkers and commuters are crawling all over the place." Without waiting for a reply, Hamilton walked towards the crime scene.

"What about the press, gov? They're going to have a fucking field day with this. Two women killed within a week and MIT have no suspects."

"Don't I know it," he replied and stopped suddenly near the forensic tent. "Now listen, Laura is already in there examining the body. I'd prefer if we could drop the charades that were played last time. Let's get the facts and get out. Understand, Lewis?"

It was more of an order than a question, but Hamilton knew Clarke wouldn't be able to resist a response. "Ah, gov, I can't help it if the opposite sex gravitates towards me. I know she still wants me. *You* know she still wants me. Hell, if she's honest with herself, she knows it too. She's just too highly strung to admit it and give in to temptation again."

Hamilton moaned as a Cheshire cat's grin appeared across his partner's face. The sun hadn't dawned on the new day, but Clarke's overconfident nature was shining through vividly. Hamilton pulled an uninterested face, his impatience growing.

"Alright, gov, your face says it all. I'll shut up. I can be professional, of course Besides, my nuts are freezing in this weather."

They both accepted the obligatory shoe covers, quickly pulled them on and made their way into the tent. Except for the blue tinge to her lips, the victim's body looked picture perfect lying on the frosty ground in a sea of dark-brown leaves. Hamilton was sure the wind would have buried her beneath the foliage if she hadn't been found so soon. Like the first victim, the body was completely naked, and he couldn't ignore that she too took pride in her appearance. Fresh highlights ran through her brunette hair. She had tanned skin and manicured, pink nails on both her hands and feet. The stem of a rose tattoo on her left hip flowed down to her pelvic bone. He imagined the flower would have peered cheekily out from her underwear just hours earlier. North of the inked artwork was a gaping blood-stained hole in her chest.

It was a tight squeeze inside the tent. Laura examined the body while two of her team members, whose names Hamilton had no interest in, scraped the victim's fingernails and took photographs. The detectives waited, but no one acknowledged them. He cleared his throat, annoyed that they were being ignored.

"Sorry, detectives, we're all busy at work here and didn't notice you," Laura said with an apologetic smile. "We set up our tent directly around the victim this morning. She hasn't been moved. We hope this, and the lack of water, will allow us to collect more evidence than the first scene did."

Hamilton jumped in before his partner could make any unwanted wisecracks. "So you think we're dealing with the same killer?"

"That's for you to determine, Denis, but my instinct tells me to answer in the positive. Yes, this woman was found in the park rather than the river, so I'm sure some of my findings will differ. But I don't think any of us can ignore the similar chest wound, or the fact that her personal belongings have been left, as before."

Clarke pulled out his notebook and pen. "So we have another name?"

"Yes, she had a driving licence in her handbag." Laura retrieved one of the plastic evidence bags from her case. "Mrs. Kate Wakeman, aged thirty-one and lived in Sloane Square. Just a fifteen-minute walk from here."

Hamilton opened the flap to leave the tent but quickly turned around to thank the pathologist, pleased that the meeting had gone more smoothly than their previous one. He was aware of how important it was to keep the peace with this team—they held vital information that could change the direction of his investigations.

"When you have a definite cause of death, or if you find anything useful from the post-mortem, please call me immediately, Laura. I want to catch this guy before he strikes again. Thank you." Hamilton walked out with Clarke in close pursuit. "It was another anonymous phone call that alerted us to the body," he explained as they crossed the park to their cars. "Call the team in. Briefing commences in one hour."

By six o'clock, the team had begun filling the incident room, most of them donning sleepy expressions. Hamilton made himself a strong cup of tea using the kettle DS Sharon Morris had set up in the corner, which held a small kitchen-style area with a mini fridge, condiments and snacks. He was always thankful of her thoughtfulness; it wasn't unusual for his team to spend late nights in the office working on a difficult case. Clarke busied himself adding information to the whiteboard; a picture of Kate Wakeman now pinned alongside Michelle Young's, their personal information underneath. Hamilton cleared his throat loudly to silence the room. Within seconds four pairs of eyes bore into him, waiting for information and instruction from their superior.

"Here's what we know. Both victims were in their late twenties, early thirties, and although we're waiting for confirmation from the post-mortem, the pathologist is confident they both died from stab wounds to the heart. The women were white, about five-foot-five or six, with long or shoulder-length brown hair and took pride in their appearance. At some point, the killer undressed the victims, but the clothing hasn't been uncovered at the scenes. Perhaps he took them to keep as souvenirs, or he's dumped them elsewhere. However, both victims were left with their handbags, and, therefore, their identification."

"What about their phones and cash? Did he take any of that with him, boss?" DS Les Wedlock called out.

Hamilton shook his head. "It's almost as if he wants us to know who the women are. He hasn't committed these crimes to mug them—quite the opposite." He paused to slurp his hot, sugary tea, leaving the room quiet and open for discussion amongst the team.

"Then perhaps there's a link between the two women. Gov, do we know if they knew each other or what their occupations were?" Morris asked.

"Good question, Sharon." Hamilton said. "Can you concentrate on that for us? Our first victim was an actress in a London theatre, and the second was a receptionist at a doctor's surgery in Pimlico. I can't see an obvious connection, but check it out. At the moment, we have no DNA evidence. There doesn't seem to have been a struggle, which makes me think that the victims knew their attacker."

He then addressed the newest recruit to the team, DS Kerry Fraser. "From what I've seen, both women looked after themselves, so perhaps they used the same gym, hairdresser, or tanning salon. Kerry, I want you to use your online skills and determine what, if anything, they had in common. And where they went in their spare time."

"I can have a look at their Facebook accounts, sir. You see, users have the option to check themselves into local places, so it's really easy to find the locations people visit regularly."

"Brilliant." He smiled, encouraged by Fraser's eagerness.

Clarke took the opportunity to remind the team of the calls received by the control room. "The reason we've uncovered the bodies so quickly, is not because we were alerted by civilians passing by, but because anonymous calls have informed us of the locations."

Hamilton raised his hand, bringing the attention back to him. "Okay, Lewis, I want you and Les to work on those calls. I'm sceptical that they were both made by frightened members of the public. So does that mean the murderer himself called us? And if the calls were made from public telephones, check if they're covered by CCTV. Oh, and one last thing, everyone… stay away from the bloody press," he said, scanning their faces. "I know the leak isn't any of you, but Christ, these vultures work fast. Let's not give them any further opportunity for information, yeah?"

The team nodded in agreement and broke off to begin their investigations. He followed Clarke to his desk and leaned in close to his partner. "I'll be in my office. I want to chase up Laura and see if there are any further developments. Let's try and get all the evidence collated as quickly as possible. We have to stop this bastard destroying a third life before the new year."

"Sure thing. And don't fret, gov, we'll nail him."

"On top of that, I have a strong feeling we're being closely watched already on this one." Clarke's eyes followed Hamilton's finger pointing to the ceiling, where his own boss, Detective Chief Inspector Allen, sat in his office above them.

CHAPTER FOUR

Daylight streamed into the bedroom and woke Grace from the alcohol-induced slumber. She felt weak, unsure how long she's been passed out, and slightly spooked by her bad dream. Although the memory of it disappeared quickly, it left a fearful aftertaste in her mind. Sheepishly, she peered over the bed, and true to her word, Valerie had cleared away the pool of sick. But a few moments later, the smell of stale vomit mixed with bleach forced Grace from her bedroom.

Downstairs, she found her mum sitting at the table in the middle of the kitchen, drinking a cup of coffee. Grace had never understood the enjoyment of the drink, and the smell, paired with her fragile stomach, made her nauseated. She covered her nose, and Valerie got up to rinse her cup in the sink.

"Have you seen the paper?" her mother asked.

"No, Mum. I think I've missed a day or two of my life, dying in bed. When would I have had time to read the paper?"

"Don't give me that tone, young lady. You weren't dying, and it was self-inflicted. I was willing to overlook your behaviour at the wake because I know how hard Granddad passing away has hit you." Valerie's face softened at the mention of her father. "But that does not mean I will accept rude sarcasm from you."

"I know, I'm sorry. I have a headache from hell, as you can imagine. I'll shake it off." Grace took a few steps across the kitchen and hugged her mum.

As always, her mum's tight embrace reassured her that everything was forgiven, and as soon as they let go of each other, her misdemeanour would be forgotten. Grace squeezed her eyes shut. She always found strength in Valerie's arms, and she needed it more than ever to get through the hangover. Grace opened her eyes and began to pull away; she felt refreshed already. But the feeling was short-lived—when the newspaper front page caught her eye, she gasped.

"Oh my God! What the hell has happened?" she squealed as she picked up the paper from the table.

"That's why I asked if you had heard the news, love. Isn't that your friend, Kate?"

She ignored her mother while she gawked at the paper, mouth wide open. She read in disbelief that Kate Wakeman was the second murder victim, just days after Michelle Young.

"Grace. Grace? Hello, I'm talking to you," Valerie called out.

Her mother's voice finally dragged her from her thoughts, and she dropped the newspaper to the floor. "What?"

"Didn't you go out drinking with that Kate girl before you went off to university?" Valerie asked, switching on the kettle.

Grace's eyes darted from side to side while her cloudy mind tried to process the information. Her thoughts were interrupted once again as the kettle bubbled and boiled, and her mother loudly clattered about making a cup of tea.

"Yes," she finally managed to answer. "We used to drink in the same pub. I suppose we were quite friendly once. Had a few heavy nights together. I just can't remember."

Valerie cut her off with a lecturing tone. "This is why young ladies shouldn't be parading themselves in the street at night. Probably, she was so drunk, she didn't even know what she was doing."

Her mum placed a steaming, strong mug of tea on the table in front of Grace, but she pushed it away. "No, Mum! Kate wasn't like that any more. Yes, we got plastered in our heyday, but she had stopped all of that behaviour. She wanted to be a nurse."

"Oh, really? How do you know that?" Valerie asked. "Had you seen her recently?"

"No. I don't think I have, actually."

"Probably that Facebook. You're all telling each other your life stories on there," Valerie continued. "But it's all just so awful.

To think, you're the same age. And just look at her photo in the paper, Grace. You both have your hair styled the same way, except she has highlights. Well, *had* highlights, I should say." Valerie paused and threw her hand over her mouth. She stared hard at Grace. "My God, look how drunk you were the other night. It could have been you! You know, I bet she was just innocently walking home that night—the paper says she lived close—and wham! You just don't know when your time is up. Except for your poor grandfather, of course. We're lucky we had a chance to say our goodbyes properly before he was completely riddled with cancer. But watching him suffer…"

Grace sucked in a deep breath. And again. And again. Her mother's speech had made her hyperventilate. She dropped to the floor in an attempt to steady her breathing. Her mother rested her hands on Grace's shoulders, but her voice sounded far off.

"Oh, my darling! I'm so sorry. I shouldn't have shown you the paper. This is all you need right now. Like you're not grieving enough."

As her eyes flooded with tears, Grace focused on Valerie's face.

"Let me get you a glass of water. It will help calm you down."

The support of her mother's hands left her, and she feared she might faint, until Valerie returned with a glass of water and placed it in front of her face. She felt the strength of her mother's grasp again.

"First Granddad and then an old friend stabbed in the street. The world isn't fair." Valerie hugged her daughter tightly to her chest and instructed her to take deep breaths. "In and out, darling. In and out."

Grace was suffocating. The once-comforting hands began to feel like a vice tightening around her. Memories filled her mind, flashed in then disappeared, making room for another glimpse of something she couldn't make out. Nothing was vivid enough for her to hold on to and remember. *This is not the time to tell Mum I also knew Michelle. I can't handle another speech.* She pulled herself up, using the granite worktop to steady her, and staggered out of the kitchen.

CHAPTER FIVE

Hamilton had never experienced any issues with his superior, Detective Chief Inspector Allen. Because he intended to keep their relationship professional, Hamilton made a point of conducting regular meetings to keep his boss abreast of the team's high-profile cases.

The DCI demanded respect as soon as he entered a room. He stood tall at six feet, two inches, and though he was in his late fifties, his thick arm and chest muscles protruded against his white fitted shirt. Although he hadn't been in a boxing ring since his mid-twenties, his physique intimidated most of his colleagues.

"It's Christmas Eve, Denis. There are two families facing the festive day without the women in their lives: their daughters, sisters, cousins, or mothers."

"Sir, neither of the women had children," Hamilton interrupted then cringed inwardly at his mistake.

"That is not my point!" Allen's voice boomed across the room.

Hamilton felt foolish. Although he had meant his comment to be light-hearted, he knew better than to be sarcastic with the chief. He had to remember he wasn't having a conversation with Clarke.

"Two families will spend their Christmas shrouded in grief, and what is it that we have to offer them, Denis? Nothing! Absolutely zilch. What is your team doing down there, dare I ask?" Allen's face turned scarlet with irritation.

Hamilton was familiar with that look of frustration because it was an emotion he battled with. But he was adamant that his team would not be held responsible for the lack of evidence. "That's unfair, sir. The entire team are working hard to find eyewitnesses, clues—anything they can use to solve this case. It's difficult, but I assure you, we will explore every avenue. A week has passed since the last murder, so yes, the trail may be lukewarm, but it's not cold yet."

Hamilton waited anxiously as the DCI closed his eyes and his huge chest sighed heavily. "What more have the pathology team told you, Denis?"

Although he didn't need his notes to prompt him—the scraps of information were secure in his memory—he preferred to look at the notebook rather than Allen's stern appearance. "We have all the information from the post-mortems, and our initial observations have been confirmed, sir: both causes of death were the stab wound to the heart. The first victim had a broken neck, but that happened after death, once she was dumped in the River Thames, Laura has informed me. The second victim's stomach contents show a high level of alcohol in her system. The family found that hard to believe as she was a recovering alcoholic and hadn't touched a drop in over five years. And no signs of sexual assault on either of the women." Hamilton looked up from his notes and waited for a response

The DCI continued to stare at him.

"Sir, we have no DNA or murder weapon," he continued, hoping his boss couldn't detect the deflated tone that was ringing bells in his own ears.

"I have to admit this is not looking good on you or the team, Denis. We may be forced to hand the investigation over if you can't produce the results. The press is already all over this, and it could turn into a very high-profile case if we're not careful. Especially if they want to spin that the Met are dragging their heels."

Hamilton didn't want to beg, but he saw the look of doubt in Allen's expression. "Please, sir, you can't do that. There aren't many clues in these cases, but we have all the information available so far. Another team would have to start right at the beginning. As I've said, we have a few more avenues to investigate. Let us see those through."

"Well, don't stop there, Denis. What are your plans?"

"DS Morris will determine where our second victim was the evening she was murdered, and we hope that will lead us to discover who she was with. DS Clarke and Wedlock have compiled a list of CCTV cameras in the vicinity of both crimes, and once they've obtained the discs, we will be giving some attention to that side of our enquiries," he replied with confidence, for his benefit as much as his superior's.

He stopped talking when Allen held up his hand. The chief rubbed his thumb and forefinger together in a circle, a telltale sign that he was deliberating over his decisions.

"Denis, I will give you until after the holidays, and then I want an arrest, or at least a damn suspect in my station. Is that clear?"

Hamilton nodded eagerly and left the office before the DCI could change his mind or add any threats.

CHAPTER SIX

G race survived Christmas in a daze, and although she hadn't suffered any nightmares, she felt numb and isolated. Regardless of the daily messages she received from her friends through WhatsApp, Facebook, and Snapchat, all trying to tempt her into attending the multitude of festive parties. The previous year, it would have been her egging other friends out for a Jäger bomb or to dance the night away.

She had visited her grandfather's grave every day and was content with wallowing in her memories. A favourite, which she couldn't ignore thinking about, was their week-long trip to Blackpool before she started secondary school. Each day on their morning stroll, her grandfather would say hello to people they passed in the street. Grace was in awe of how many friends he had, even in a seaside town she had never visited before.

"I'm just being friendly," her grandfather had laughed in reply when she asked how he knew everyone. His strong Cork accent still sounded clear in her mind.

She thought about the massive ice-cream cones they had shared as they sat on the pier; he'd regularly recollected the memory even some twenty years after their visit.

Valerie's voice pulled Grace from her sweet musings as she pottered about the kitchen, making tea. "Darling, you have to go and socialise. It's New Year's Eve, and all your friends miss you."

"Mum, I really don't feel like celebrating. Surely you can understand that! Besides, I'm back to work next week, and I want a clear head. I've got so much to catch up on. The theatre will showcase a new performance this year, and I have no idea what's going on."

"They all understand why you've had some time off."

"Mum!" Grace interrupted. She exhaled deeply through her nose and clenched her teeth. "Don't talk about grief again."

She made her frustration obvious, hoping her mother would take the hint and back off from the subject.

"I just meant, yes you've missed out on some things because of your compassionate leave, but you're brilliant at what you do. It won't take you long to catch up. I have faith in you."

"Seriously, I don't need a pep talk, Mum." She sighed.

"It's hard for all of us. We've all lost a man from our lives that was so loving, strong, and influential. Albeit stubborn." Valerie laughed gently, in an obvious ploy to lighten the atmosphere, but Grace knew it was far too late for that.

"Mum," she said sharply, her eyes wide and glaring. "I'm fine. I just don't fancy going to any New Year's Eve party. Now please, drop this conversation."

"Maybe you could talk to someone. You know, like a counsellor-type person. I'd be happy to go with you. I mean, first your grandfather and then your poor friend brutally murdered. It's horrific what you're going through."

"Stop!" Grace bellowed at the top of her voice, her face burning and her hands balled into fists. "I don't need to talk to anyone. I have nothing to say. Do you understand? I have nothing to say."

She swung round and smacked the cup of tea off the kitchen table. She was already out of the room when the white mug connected with the floor and smashed into pieces.

****

Valerie tapped lightly on the door and waited. When no answer came, she debated taking the mug of tea back downstairs. A few hours had passed since their last scene, and she thought perhaps Grace had fallen asleep. She soon detected the light sound of sobs from the other side of the door and quietly pushed it open, peering in.

Sitting cross-legged on her butterfly-design bedspread, Grace held her head in her hands. Her long, dark hair fell around her, and she was weeping. A large pink box was open, and she knew that meant Grace had been looking through old photographs. She placed the mug of tea on the bedside table and lowered herself onto the bed. Without saying a word, she wrapped her arms around her daughter and looked down at the photographs. Spread around them were years of memories shared with their beloved departed. They sat, embraced on the bed, for what seemed like hours, but Valerie wouldn't let go. She wanted Grace to know she was there to support her. They cried together, and when there were no more tears left, they sat in silence. Eventually, the ache of their pins and needles became too much to bear, and they were forced to pull apart.

"I'm sorry," Grace whispered, as Valerie watched her listless daughter search for a tissue. Her nose was blocked, and her red eyes bulged.

"Don't apologise. I know that I shouldn't keep pushing you to talk to someone that you don't want to. It's not my place. We all deal with things differently."

"But I am sorry," Grace repeated as she stared down at her fumbling fingers. "I mean, I know I should say sorry. I feel I should. I just don't always remember what I'm saying it for."

Valerie put her arm around her daughter's shoulders when she noticed Grace's eyes had filled with tears once again.

"Mum, I know sometimes I snap at you for the most trivial things. But afterwards, I can't even remember what it was I said, and then… and then, I don't know. I feel so drained." The tears escaped again.

"It's grief, darling. Please don't worry. Lie down and get some rest." Valerie helped Grace lower herself onto the pillow then covered her with a blanket.

From the bedroom door, she turned to watch her adult daughter lie silently like a small child. How she always thought Grace looked when she slept.

CHAPTER SEVEN

The rustle of leaves alerted her to someone following close by. She stopped still, staring into the bushes, urging her eyes to adjust to the shadows. The park was gloomy. Thick black clouds covered the brightness of the full moon, and useless streetlamps flickered, failing to fully light the pavement in front of her. She picked up speed as the wind whistled around her and the cold breeze hit hard against her bare skin. She cursed her decision not to add a coat to her skimpy red bodycon dress. She stumbled in her black stilettos as she walked through the empty playground.

She screeched, her body jerked, and she dropped her handbag. *Jesus, it's way after midnight. What's wrong with these pricks?*

The banging and popping of the fireworks frustrated her—they inhibited her ability to listen for the footsteps she was sure had crept by. When the last rocket soared and fizzled out in the sky, the park was alarmingly quiet and shrouded in shadows again. She held her breath, scanning furiously from side to side, but it was impossible to see anything in the darkness. Exhaling slowly, she contemplated reaching for her phone, but was frozen in fear, incapable of bending down to retrieve it. Something cold swept against her exposed arm, and she bolted for the exit in a daze, fueled by alcohol and adrenaline.

She drew closer to the gate, trying to run faster, but the heel of her shoe caught in the shingles of the pavement, tossing her face-first onto the gravel. Her hands were grazed, specks of blood mixed with grit, and she grunted in pain turning onto her side.

Heavy footsteps skimmed along the concrete, taunting her with their slow advance. Her heart beat furiously. She wanted to get up and run—the gate was so close. But her brain wasn't reacting to her commands. It was too late.

The silhouette stopped at her feet, and the tall figure bent over her. She opened her mouth to scream, but the wind caught her breath and took it in the breeze. The hooded figure inched closer to her.

"Fuck! What are you doing? You scared the shit out of me!" She sighed and lifted her right arm in the air. "Well, bloody help me up then," she continued to yelp.

In that moment, the glint of the blade caught her eye. Seconds later, she felt the cold knife edge enter her chest, piercing her heart.

CHAPTER EIGHT

G race stood in the shower, eyes closed and head resting against the tiles. She yearned for more sleep, but her mind focused on the visions that had pulled her from her sleep once again. Surrounded by the darkness, women's screams resonated in her ears, and the odd flash of colour, a deep red or rusty brown, filled her memory. She couldn't keep her eyes closed for long before the anxiety returned and the breathlessness took over. Standing directly under the showerhead, Grace attempted to ignore her thoughts. She allowed the hot water to wash over her, beat down onto her face. She wanted it to erase the images from her mind. It was her first day back to work after two weeks, and Grace worried she had adopted the look of a banshee.

The underground journey into Central London felt exactly as it had before, except for old train acquaintances wishing each other best wishes for the New Year. Grace paid no attention to them and happily sat in an overcrowded carriage with strangers, their heads buried deep in The Metro, avoiding eye contact. Something captured her attention, and she edged forward on her seat to read the newspaper held up by the man opposite.

"I know that story," she said, forgetting where she was for a moment.

"That's no story!" a large redheaded lady to her left answered. "That poor woman was found on New Year's Day. Murdered like the others, except her clothes were left on. They've dubbed her the Lady in Red. Isn't it awful? Us women can't even walk home safely in our own city without fear of what could happen to us," the woman roared as though she were addressing the whole train, and a shiver tingled down Grace's spine.

She hopped off the train at her station and automatically followed the swarm of commuters to the exit. The fresh air was a welcome wake-up call as she walked the short distance to work. Standing in front of the theatre, Grace sighed. Her eyes roamed over the grand building and lingered on the bold lettering of their new play: *The Lady in Red*.

"That needs to change, right?" a voice whispered in her ear.

There was no need to turn around. The clean, fresh smell of Calvin Klein filled her nostrils, and goosebumps swept over her body.

Eric walked round her and offered his arms out for an embrace. Grace gladly fell against his warm chest.

"How are you?" He asked, his warm breath tickling over her bare neck.

That's a new tartan scarf. Christmas present from his mum. I hope. She pulled away and looked into his warm hazel eyes. "I'm fine. So please, spread the word to cut the sympathy act. I just want to get back to normal now." Grace couldn't hold his gaze.

"Yes, ma'am." Eric mock-saluted and nudged her shoulder. "Well, your first order of business is to find a new name for that," he said, pointing to the sign above the theatre door. "No one is going to come and see a play named after a dead woman."

"Who came up with the name?" she whispered.

"I did. Well, we all did, as a team. Don't you remember, before your... before you... left. Well, you know, before..."

"Before my grandad died? You can say it, Eric. And no, actually, I don't remember."

****

Michael Sparks had headhunted Grace when he opened his theatre three years ago in Covent Garden. Her reputation of being organised, meticulous, and inspirational to those she worked with had preceded her, and ultimately secured her the job as assistant director at The London.

Grace's love of the theatre was obvious to Michael. He knew of her ambition to become a famous actress, to dominate the stages and fascinate audiences everywhere with her talents. When they first met, she told him that she was in awe of the stage, thrilled to watch actors become someone new and bring that character's story to life. He remembered every word she'd uttered. Sadly, the dramatic life was not to be for Grace, who forgot lines, tripped over props, and froze in front of an audience of more than ten people. Desperate to not leave the stage completely, she'd started as a runner and worked her way to the top, gaining a wealth of knowledge and experience from a variety of theatres, in a range of different jobs. Michael knew that he needed Grace Murphy on his team. She was a highly respected go-getter willing to try her hand at any role to create a successful theatre.

"We need a meeting. Now!" Grace stood at his office door, her hands placed firmly on her hips.

"Erm… Good morning. Happy New Year. Welcome back. Nice to see you. Any of those could also work," Michael replied, smiling.

"Our new play is called *The Lady in Red*. A murdered woman has today been given that name in the press. We need a meeting, Michael. Now. I'll get the room ready."

He felt giddy as Grace marched away from him. His chest heaved with happiness that this feisty brunette was back in her rightful place at the theatre. He'd expected nothing less of her than the passionate entrance he'd just witnessed, happy for her to take the lead role in their working relationship, despite him being the director.

Michael watched her in awe. She was a mystery to him. She had a passionate and energetic side, but he had also witnessed a reserved and shy character that she sometimes adopted. *Oh how I long to get into her mind. Into her mind, and her body.* Dragged back to reality, a frustrated Michael stared down the corridor towards Grace and Eric. Her hand grazed the man's masculine biceps.

Last year, Michael hired Eric as lead male because of his outstanding experience and stunning references. Watching the pair, he winced as his perfect leading lady flirted with the six-foot-tall, tanned man he'd welcomed into The London.

"Hello!" Despite its high-pitched yell, her voice sang to him. "Can we get a move on, Michael? We have some important decisions to make and not a lot of time to do it in."

CHAPTER NINE

The meeting kept Grace busy for most of her first day back at work, and she was thrilled to be part of the team again. When she finally checked her phone, after shutting down her computer to leave, she was greeted with a number of missed calls and messages. She opened WhatsApp and found the unread messages from Natasha, her best friend since high school.

Natasha: OMFG!!! It's your first day back at work. Sorry I didn't call last night. Meet me tonight for a drink. It's been sooooo long, and we need a catch up. Pls xx

Grace read the message and sighed at the thought of the carefree days. She often met her friend in the pub, at least once a week, but since her grandfather passed away she'd barely even spoken to her. They usually joked and called it their own version of the Monday Club, because they never ditched work first—they were professional women. She was always in awe of Natasha's feisty, laid-back attitude. With her flame-red hair and several tattoos, most people thought it odd when they discovered a spirited individual such as Natasha was a solicitor at a top London firm. Grace knew working in a male-dominated arena was part of the attraction for her friend, but Natasha also enjoyed proving the haters wrong and was a fierce opponent in the courtroom.

Natasha: I miss u xx

She felt a pang of guilt as she read the second message on her phone. She didn't want to suffer a night of sympathy and questions, but she couldn't exclude her friends any more. Empowered by a day of making tough decisions, changing the production name, and editing advertising material, Grace replied.

Grace: Meet u @ The Oak in an hour x

The Royal Oak—or the Oak, as they called it—was a local pub in their hometown of Brent. They had met in that very pub when they were underage drinkers at seventeen, and even while they were living in halls at university, they regularly travelled back on weekends to catch up with friends. Most pubs in the area had closed down, and their friends had moved and bought homes in Radlett or Harlow to begin families. Grace loved living at home with her mum and having that sense of community around her. Even though both women earned good money, they preferred having a beer at the local pub, rather than drinking cocktails with names they couldn't pronounce, in Central London wine bars.

Eager to chat over a cold glass of San Miguel, Grace quickly made her way through the dark corridor leading to the small offices, each of which was large enough for only a table and a filing cabinet. The larger rooms, where the activity was livelier, were used for dressing rooms, costumes and props. Stunned by the bang as she passed Michael's office, she stiffened and waited for another sound. In the eerie silence of the corridor, her hand trembled over the door handle. Her gut told her to flee the darkness, but as always, her enquiring mind won. From behind the desk, Eric looked up at her with a solemn expression, and she sensed a genuine sadness in his otherwise-beautiful hazel eyes.

"Shit! What the hell are you doing in here?" Grace screeched, leaning on the doorframe.

"Sorry," he replied, but he didn't make eye contact with her.

"You scared me. It's so dark in the corridor. I heard a loud bang, and then it went quiet. Plus, I knew Michael had already gone home," she rambled, attempting to shake the fright she'd just had.

But Eric obviously wasn't paying much attention, as he didn't look up from the glass he held lightly in his hand. Grace had never witnessed him in this mood, and she was unsure of what to say. *I know what I'd like to do. If I could just straddle him on that chair…*

"I'm sorry. I dropped the bottle of whiskey. Luckily, it didn't break." Eric's voice distracted her from her lustful thoughts. "I saw Michael leave too. I know he always keeps some of this stuff in the office, so I thought, 'Why not?'" he continued, shaking the Jameson bottle.

"You don't look like you're in the mood for a drink," Grace said, suddenly remembering her own plans.

A moment of silence lingered before she began to feel guilty. "I'm sorry, Eric. I really have to leave. I'm supposed to be—"

"Please don't leave me. I could really use a friend right now."

He finally looked at her, devouring her with his watery eyes. The sadness in them called to her like a wounded puppy vying for attention.

"Oh, Eric. I wish I could. It's just—"

"I've missed you these past few weeks. Our drinks after work. Our chats. I could really do with those things right now. With you."

But he'd had her full attention at "I've missed you," and she knew exactly what her next move would be.

Although nothing romantic had ever happened between them, she always wondered if it were possible. And if she was honest with herself, she knew from the moment she'd opened the door and seen Eric's face that she wasn't meeting Natasha. *I'll send her an apologetic message quickly. If I explain, she'll understand.* It wasn't the first time Grace had changed her plans for him.

CHAPTER TEN

The door slammed shut with such force, the detectives stopped what they were doing and watched Hamilton storm through the incident room. "Who the fuck is leaking this information to the press?" He caught Fraser flinch. The newest member of his team hadn't witnessed his temper, but he was damned if he was going to apologise.

"The chief is fuming," he bellowed while pacing the room. "They've dubbed our third victim 'the Lady in Red' because she was still fully clothed. Where in God's name do they get all these bloody facts?" Hamilton didn't give his team time to answer before he strode off into his office in the corner of the incident room.

The shrill of the telephone startled him, and still raging from his outburst, he forcefully snatched the receiver. "What?"

"Doesn't sound like you're having a great day, Inspector."

He wasn't amused with the sarcastic comment from the caller, but he endeavoured to calm down as he recognised the voice.

"I was just about to call you, Laura, and no, it has not been a good day. Actually, it hasn't been a bloody good start to the year." The anger was quickly replaced with self-doubt, and Hamilton slumped into his chair. "I need to catch this guy."

"I'm sorry to hear the disappointment in your voice, Denis. But I do have some details about your latest victim."

Hamilton smiled at the sound of her genuine tone. He had heard through the grapevine that Laura spent years studying, to the detriment of her own social life, to become an expert in her field. With long blonde hair and an athletic body, she often received unwanted attention while working in a male-dominated profession. He respected her for using her knowledge to outwit some of the sleazebags she had to call colleagues and climb the ladder to become head pathologist.

"Brilliant, Laura. I'm all ears."

"Okay, your victim is twenty-eight-year-old Vicky Lawlor. I've just sent the post-mortem report to you via e-mail, but in short, the cause of death is the same as your first two victims: stab wound directly through the heart. No DNA on the body or clothes."

"Why leave her clothes on?" Hamilton thought aloud.

"It was New Year's Eve. Maybe he was just disturbed," Laura offered. "He stuck to his type: a brunette, petite, beautiful woman who looked after herself. So I'd guess it wasn't a random attack. But maybe he slipped up and didn't appreciate how many people would be on the street at that time of the morning."

"Playing detective, are we?" Hamilton asked light-heartedly.

"I'm a straight-up facts and DNA kind of girl, you know that. I'm just throwing in an observation."

"But what if he wasn't disturbed? Thanks, Laura. You've given me a new viewpoint to think about. Speak soon."

They ended the call, and Hamilton rushed back into the incident room. His haste had the desired effect—his team embraced his newfound excitement and rallied around him as he added notes to the whiteboard.

"Why the change in mood, gov?" Clarke asked.

"I don't think her clothes were left on because he was disturbed by a passer-by, Lewis. I think he's sending us a message." He turned to face the team and was pleased to have gained their full attention.

Hamilton finished adding the victim's name to the whiteboard before he continued with his theory. It built an air of excitement in the room, and he loved it. "If he was interrupted by a partygoer, surely they would have called it in and stuck around for the police, as most people do. But this murderer stuck to the same MO, and we received the anonymous tip-off. I think it's him tipping us off. He wants us to find the bodies quickly, and he obviously wants us to know who the victims are straight away. We just have to find out why."

"So her clothes are just another message?" Fraser asked.

"Yes, I think so, Kerry. Maybe this one was more personal than the others."

"Perhaps this Vicky was in on it from the beginning, went rogue on him, and he took his revenge," Wedlock shouted out.

"That's what we're going to find out," Hamilton replied. "Lewis, I want us to pay a visit to Vicky Lawlor's family. I just need to update the DCI first. Here's the post-mortem report, Sharon. Have a look at it and see if anything catches your eye; Laura doesn't seem to think so, but I don't want anything left uncovered. Les and Kerry, I want a full background search of our victim—everything from where she worked down to who her friends were. This could be the break in the case we needed. Let's get to work!" Hamilton clapped his hands, and the energy surged into his team as they rushed to fulfil their tasks.

"Lewis, I'll meet you in the car." Hamilton bombed out of the office and made his way upstairs to see his superior. He hoped this new direction would give him extra time on a case he was worried could slip out of his hands.

CHAPTER ELEVEN

The memory of her cocktail session with Eric reignited feelings of excitement that Grace hadn't felt for months. But a bittersweet taste to the evening lingered when she recalled the reason for Eric's sadness. He spoke of a woman he had been dating casually—Grace had quickly dubbed her "the bitch"—who had betrayed him. She was glad he didn't want to talk further about the relationship or what the other woman had done. After an enjoyable evening in a local bar, Grace and Eric said goodnight at the tube station—not the end to the evening she had hoped for, but it was the professional one to make.

She shook her thoughts away and looked at the clock on her office wall: six o'clock. *That's enough overtime for one day.* Plus, it was Friday, and no one stayed late on the weekends when there wasn't a performance. They'd pushed back the opening date after choosing a new working title, and in the meantime, new advertising material was being produced. She and Michael hoped the media would ignore the change. The crew used the delay as an excuse to rush out into the streets of London looking for fun, and Grace supposed it was about time she rejoined her own friends. *I'll message Natasha, see if she'll meet me for a drink and make up for my faux pas earlier in the week.*

She was keen not to keep the caretaker much longer, as it was his job to lock up the theatre, so she hurried to her office to collect her belongings. She took the shortcut, along the back of the stage, but stopped suddenly when she heard movement and voices from beyond the main stage area. Certain she was on her own, she crept slowly towards the heavy black curtains, shocked to hear a woman giggling. Grace sighed with relief upon realising there was no threat, but curiosity got the better of her. She edged closer to the stage, using the curtains as a shield, and peeped through the opening gap in the middle. What she witnessed stunned her.

Eric's strong, masculine body pinned Emily against the wall. She laughed and wrapped her legs tighter around his waist. Her short black skirt inched farther up her thighs. Eric's hand followed the material until his fingers crept underneath it, and she groaned. Spurred on by the moans, Eric unbuttoned Emily's white shirt and buried his face in her ample breasts, pushed her bra away with his lips and sucked her nipples; the woman threw her head back in ecstasy. His lips glided to her neck, and his hands gripped tightly around Emily's waist. In one swift movement, Eric pulled her from the wall and forcefully placed her down on one of the speakers. He stood between her legs, and Grace could sense his hunger as he furiously untied his belt and trousers.

Astonished by what she was watching, Grace couldn't look away. Eric pushed his trousers to the floor, reached under Emily's skirt, and ripped off her knickers before diving back down to kiss her breasts. Breathing heavily, Emily groaned and thrashed her head from side to side. Grace realised she had been caught spying on them when Emily's head lingered to the left briefly, followed by exaggerated groans and a slight chuckle. Embarrassed, Grace stumbled backwards and ran off down the corridor.

Her hands quivered as she attempted to shut down her computer, collect her bag, and lock her office door. To avoid the stage, she took the longer route towards the exit, but her efforts were in vain as Emily stood brazenly in the hallway, adjusting her shirt in the mirror.

"Enjoy the show, you perv?"

"Don't talk to me like that. I'm the assistant director of this theatre." But Grace's whispering tone and crimson cheeks drowned her confident words. She tried to walk past Emily, but the woman refused to move.

"Gracie, we all know you like Eric. I guess he just prefers blondes." Emily mocked her with a flick of her curly, long hair and a deep laugh that made her shudder. The women glared at each other. Standing four inches above Grace's petite physique, Emily looked down at her with cold blue eyes. She feared Emily would use the situation against her for a long time to come.

"Oh! Hi, ladies. Is everything okay?" Eric asked after he appeared in the hallway with Michael.

Neither woman answered him. Emily looked at their boss, and for a brief moment, Grace thought the shameless hussy looked uncomfortable.

"I didn't realise you were still here, Michael," Emily finally said.

"Oh, you know, just doing some research," Michael replied, his face firmly fixed on Grace's. "It's been a long week, what with the changes to the play and everything. Grace, is everything okay?"

"Yes. Fine. Must dash." She spun round and power-walked up the steep stairs to the main entrance.

She swung the door open and gulped in the cold air. Not wishing to get involved in a further confrontation with her colleagues, she ran to the side alley and made sure they passed her first before she left. Grace shook as she reached inside her handbag for her iPhone and tried to use her thumbprint to access the phone. Her skin was too sweaty for it to work. She cursed as she entered the four-digit code and opened WhatsApp.

Grace: Tash, pls meet me @ The Oak in an hour. I need a drink. An XL drink! U won't believe what I have just seen!!!! x

CHAPTER TWELVE

The Oak was dated, and Grace couldn't remember it ever being renovated. That was part of its charm with the regulars: it felt like a second home. Although it had only one entrance, the pub was distinctively halved. The walls of the top bar were covered with black-and-white photographs of the area from the fifties and sixties. Old punters propped themselves up against the bar or played cards. The bottom bar enticed the younger generation with a pool table and jukebox. A few odd football scarves were plastered all around the area in a bid to inject some colour on the beige walls. The weekends threw away that divide when the pub welcomed its resident DJ, who played popular tunes from his booth in the bottom bar.

Pleased to see Natasha waiting with two large glasses of white wine, Grace rushed over to her friend.

"I'm going to skate pass the fact that you dumped me on Monday because: one, you were with Eric, and he's hot. And two, it sounds like you have some juicy gossip."

"I wasn't *with him* with him. It was just a few drinks and a chat." Grace gulped a mouthful of wine. "But all that doesn't matter because I just caught him having sex on the stage at work."

"What do you mean? As in a rehearsal for a play or something? Oh, maybe I will come and see that one then."

Grace almost choked laughing at her friend. "No, Natasha! Not for the bloody play. Would I be shocked if that was the case? I caught him having actual real-life, sneaky sex with Emily." She lifted her eyebrows, and her lips turned up at the corners.

"What the fuck!" Natasha screamed over the music. "Emily, as in the little runner girl at the theatre? The tart, you mean?"

She took another swig of wine. "The one and only, yes. Disgusting, right? My mind keeps seeing them together. Urgh! I hope this wine kicks in soon. And after everything he said to me on Monday. 'Oh, Grace, she's hurt me so much,' and 'I can't believe I was taken in by her.' What a load of bullshit. Men!" Grace added an exaggerated shiver and screwed up her face, making Natasha laugh.

The two women fell back into easy conversation and jokes despite the fact that they hadn't seen each other in over a month. Grace replenished their drinks, opting to buy a bottle of wine for them to share. As the evening progressed, the pub became crowded and the DJ hitched up the bass on his sound system. Natasha suggested they go outside. Although the smokers' garden seemed just as busy, it had a calming atmosphere that came from strangers engaged in general chit-chat about life in a nicotine-welcomed daze. The pair only smoked when they were drunk, and Grace was ready for the occasion. She pulled a ten-pack of Mayfair from her handbag, took out two cigarettes, gave one to her friend, and lit the other for herself. She inhaled deeply, and the head rush caused a dull in her mood.

"Oh, Natasha! I feel so strange all the time."

"You need to get laid, my friend. That's the problem." Natasha cackled and glanced round the garden.

Grace rolled her eyes, knowing her friend was on the hunt for men. "No, no, no! You don't understand. I'm having these awful dreams. I mean, when I wake up, I don't really remember much of them, but they make me feel scared. Then all these murders are happening. And I knew two of the girls. Well, actually, Natasha, you did too. Doesn't it scare you?"

"It's horrifying times we live in. Yes, we knew them a long time ago, but you have to understand that there's so much violence in this city alone, it's bound to affect everyone at some point in their lives. Sadly, every murder victim out there is someone's friend. You know there are teenagers out there on the street, killing each other? Well, my sister went to school with a lad that was shot in a club last week. There was no fight or argument, and he died instantly. And with that, they leave a wake of people that knew them at some stage in their life. It's terrifying to think about what crazies are walking the streets."

Natasha drank her wine while Grace thought about what her friend had said. Thinking of more crimes being committed close to home actually didn't help.

"But really listen, babe, maybe you need to see a shrink. I find it easy to compartmentalise these horrendous crimes because of my job. It sounds like you have some bottled-up emotions and they're taking root in your dreams. You should seek out some professional help," Natasha said, but her attention was now fixed on a group of men a few tables away.

As she reached for another cigarette, Grace sighed at her friend's suggestion and lack of attentiveness. She was desperate to talk more about her nightmares with Natasha, but she was interrupted when a striking blond man at least six feet tall approached their table.

"Hiya, ladies. I'm Ben, and that's my friend, Nicky." The stranger gestured to the handsome man with spikey brown hair, who peered over from his seat, obviously not as brave as this guy.

"Can we buy you both a drink?" Ben asked.

"Two white wines, please." Natasha gave her best dazzling smile.

Grace smirked at the guy and pulled at Natasha's jacket, leaning close to her friend's ear. "Erm… hello, I thought we were having a chat?"

"Yes, we have chatted. It's been great, just like old times. So let's continue with that and have a bloody laugh. These two are hotties, and they're not regulars. They could be fun."

"I don't want to have fun with these strangers. I wanted to have a heart-to-heart with my best friend, about something really serious I'm going through. I could use *your* help with it, not a random shrink," she said, screwing up her face.

"And I can totally understand that, Grace. But seriously, come on now. It's Friday night. It's time to live, feel young and free. We can catch up about all this other stuff in the week." Natasha turned her attention back to Ben, giggled, and stroked his huge muscles bulging through his tight black T-shirt.

Grace could feel the tears rise to her eyes as her friend dismissed her, but refusing to feel weak, she pushed them back and drained her glass of wine.

She staggered out of the pub alone. Without the halogen heaters from the smokers' garden, the fierce wind hit her hard in the face, and she lowered her head to walk against it. The taxi office on the corner, which had always offered a safe journey home for the patrons of The Oak, had shut down before Christmas. Grace cursed her forgetfulness but refused to return to the pub. She knew that Natasha and the guys would be in full flirting mode, and she had no interest in entertaining that.

In a drunken stupor, Grace sauntered down the high street in search of an alternative route home. *Perhaps I could catch the night bus.* But the silent street encouraged her mind to wander to other things, thoughts of Eric and Emily being at the forefront. She felt foolish for flirting with him and believing his sob story. The cold January breeze continued to bash her, and she stumbled into the shutters of a closed bakery. The distance between her and the blaring music from the pub had increased; it had become nothing but a faint thud. Desperate to find another taxi office, she walked faster, but couldn't ignore the sound of footsteps echoing behind her.

All the shops were shut, most covered by graffitied iron shutters. The street was dimly lit, and shadows frolicked around her on the ground. Panic set in. She began running along the pavement, the sound of her breathing vibrated in her ears. Her high heels awkwardly slapped against the concrete, and the noise echoed the length of the road. She was too afraid to turn around. *Oh God! Why did I leave the pub alone?* She bolted round the corner so fast, she didn't notice the towering figure dressed head to toe in black, and ran directly into his solid frame. A piercing scream escaped her lips, and she cowered. *I'm going to die tonight.*

"Grace! Grace!"

Relief washed over her when she peeped through her fingers and saw Eric standing in front of her. She threw her arms around his waist and stayed in that position for a few minutes, calming her erratic breathing in his safe hold.

"Grace, why are you running through Neasden high street at this time of night? You must know this park is a hunting area for local gangs."

Safe in her mind that she could finally let go of Eric without falling over, she released his waist and noticed he was right. If he hadn't stopped her, she would have run straight into Royals Park, a notorious stomping ground for muggers. She suddenly remembered the footsteps that had followed her and forced her to take flight. Spinning round, she scanned the street, frosty air passing through her lips. But the thick darkness of the night covered everything. The odd tree cast a fluttering shadow, but no one was there.

"I left the Oak and thought someone was chasing me. I couldn't remember where the closest taxi office was. What are you doing here? I mean, thank God you are—you stopped me blindly entering that park. What a fool I am." She feared her drunken babble and flustered appearance would be a complete turn off to him.

"Yeah, running towards that hellhole probably wasn't your smartest move to date, babe."

Eric's choice of endearment affected her; the pit of her stomach somersaulted, and her earlier doubts about him disappeared. He slid his arm around her shoulders and she contentedly allowed him to lead her away from the park entrance.

"Well, you obviously haven't had enough alcohol tonight." He chuckled, and she snuggled closer under his arm. "Come back to mine, and we'll have a drink together."

CHAPTER THIRTEEN

I stalked her, spied on her through the trees, hidden in the darkness. She was obviously pissed—she could barely walk in a straight line. *This will be easy.* She continued to wiggle her arse as she walked, exuding confidence and a flirtatious attitude. Even when she thought she was alone, she was a cocky bitch. It was about time she learnt taunting people with her sexiness, as if she were the most important person in the world. This was not something I enjoyed watching.

She entered the iron gates of the park, the *perfect* place for what I had planned. I was concealed by the shadows because of the council's unwillingness to replace broken lamps. *Lucky for me it's a shitty town.* The winter chill raged around her, and she burrowed down into her expensive-looking beige coat. Twigs snapped under her four-inch stilettos; the leaves rustled in a mini whirlwind close to the ground. The sound of her heels clicked and scraped the pavement, driving me insane. My anger grew, the closer she came. She ridiculed innocent people. How fucking dare she? *I'm the only one powerful enough to stop this, to put her in place.*

The exit gate was closed, and I laughed as her pace quickened. The park was even darker there. I pounced from behind the shrubs. She shrieked, and a rush of adrenaline surged through my body. It felt good to be in control again. Her eyes were wide in fear, the colour had drained from her skin, and she was desperate to scream. But she didn't—or couldn't. I didn't care which. The domination was exhilarating. My dark clothes and hood concealed my identity as always.

She was distracted for a split second, peering at my gloved hands. The glint caught her eyes. I lunged, knocking her to the ground, silencing her cry for help. Straddling her waist, I strapped her arms to her side with my thighs and covered her mouth with my free hand. Her face showed the fear and pain. It was euphoric. She thrashed about under me; it must have been painful.

She focused on me, her captor, and I saw a spark of recognition. Her eyes widened, and a panicked squeal escaped from under the glove.

"Yes, it's me." I smiled, so she would know I was enjoying myself, and ran the blade along her cheek. She didn't move. The knife glided farther, and the cold metal caressed her bare skin until it reached the top of her blouse.

"You really should be careful who you tease. It's not nice to upset people I care about. I don't like it." The blade rested on her chest.

She swallowed loudly. Her fear sent me into a frenzy, and the authority made my skin tingle.

I released her mouth but gave her no time to scream out. In one swift movement, I clutched her hair tight in my fist, yanked her head inches from the ground, and smashed it down onto the concrete path. Blood seeped from the back of her head. Her eyes glazed over.

"Don't leave the party just yet."

I wrapped both hands around the handle and plunged the knife straight through her heart. Full of rage, I did it again and again and again. There was blood everywhere—it matched the release flowing within my body. I stood up and looked down at her lifeless body.

"I'll leave your clothes on, you filthy slut. Too many people have seen you naked already."

CHAPTER FOURTEEN

Grace felt the crisp white sheets slide across her naked skin before she opened her eyes. *Oh shit!* She found the courage to open her eyes and quickly scanned the foreign bedroom she had woken in. Perplexed, she contemplated where she was and what the nightmare haunting her meant this time.

"Well, good morning, you." Eric appeared at the doorway wearing only his boxer shorts.

Grace briefly closed her eyes, and her memory was jolted with images of a dark street, naked bodies, a kitchen table, and a full moon. She squinted and rubbed her temples.

"Did we…?" She opened her eyes just in time to see Eric's cheeks blush slightly and a hint of a smirk.

"We did. And I must say, Grace—wow! You're a firecracker." He chuckled at her confused expression. "I would have never expected it from you. I always thought you were quite timid, you know. But after we got back here and had a few more drinks, it was like you were on heat. You were all over me, and to be honest, it was difficult to resist. It got a bit intense in the kitchen, and we did it on the table, and then again on the stairs before we finally made it in here and collapsed." He laughed again, animated with his story as he walked into the room. "It was sexy, Grace. I've never seen you so full of passion. You should let that side out more." He winked and waltzed off to the en-suite bathroom.

She cringed, embarrassed by how Eric spoke about her. She wanted to run away as fast as possible and hide. *I guess that explains the dream.* She inspected the room again. The king-size bed took up most of the space, and she was surprised there were no personal photos, but the dressing table held a large vanity mirror adorned with small lightbulbs. Beech-coloured french blinds kept prying eyes out of the huge bay windows behind the dressing table. *Very classy, not like my nets and heavy curtains.* Clothing was strewn over the white, fluffy carpet; Grace lifted the duvet and got out of the bed to retrieve her clothes and cover her naked body.

"So listen." Eric peered round the bathroom door, forcing her to pull the cover back over her. "I really enjoyed myself last night, Grace. Seriously, you were awesome, and it was fun. But…"

She could feel him struggling with the end of his sentence. Her face was on fire. *Shit, could this be any more embarrassing?* "Eric, don't worry. No one will find out about this."

He responded with a goofy smile and stuck his thumb up before returning to the bathroom. Shame washed over her as she searched the floor for her clothes. After throwing on her black skirt and bra, she raced downstairs to find her panties and shirt in the kitchen. Once dressed, she paused in front of the large hallway mirror and looked intently at her shabby reflection. Horror and disappointment simultaneously crowded her mind, and she took flight from Eric's apartment.

The fresh morning chill hit Grace's face as she strolled home. She knew the wise thing would be to jump in a taxi, rush home, and hide away for the weekend, but she wanted to clear her hangover and bemused thoughts. She turned onto her road twenty minutes later and slumped in despair as her neighbour walked out of his front gate and turned towards her. Her mind scrambled. Should she turn back and hope he hadn't seen her? Maybe she could power-walk past him as if she were in a rush? When he lifted his hand and waved in her direction, she realised neither of those scenarios would work. She groaned inside, gave in to fate, and plastered a fake smile on her face.

"Good morning, Grace," Mr. Wilson said.

He walked swiftly towards her. She dreaded that he wouldn't stop until his nose was touching hers.

"Good morning, and hello, Simba." Grace bent down, more in attempt to regain her personal space than to stroke the German shepherd.

"I'm just taking the bitch for a morning walk," he complained.

She cringed at his lack of affection and gave the dog some extra attention.

"So, you're not usually out and about this early on the weekend. Stayed over with a friend, eh?" Mr. Wilson winked mischievously, making her shudder.

"Yes, I did," she replied as she stood up, keen to keep their conversation short.

"Really? Male or female?"

"Does that matter, Mr. Wilson?"

He laughed, mouth wide open, displaying teeth discoloured by years of smoking. Actually, she was surprised he didn't have a tobacco stick hanging from his mouth, as he usually did.

"Come now, don't be shy. Neighbours share gossip when they bump into each other, don't they?"

"I wouldn't really know," she snapped, irritated by his assumption.

"No, I guess you wouldn't. I've noticed you don't tend to venture out much any more. Since your grandfather died, I mean. Shame that was. He was a decent guy. Always gave me a ciggie when I tapped him up for one. But I only see you heading in and out to work now, not a lot of partying in your skimpy outfits any more, not like you used to. Except for last night maybe, eh." He winked again and prodded her arm lightly with this elbow.

Grace felt enraged that a married man in his late forties would speak to her in such a way. She squashed the urge to slap his face, knowing the scene would cause her mum embarrassment in the neighbourhood.

"I think it's quite rude to speculate on my life, Mr. Wilson." She watched the grin slip from his face.

He frowned but remained quiet.

"What I do in my private life is exactly that—*private*," she said, uncomfortable with the prolonged silence.

He leered. "I was just making polite chit-chat, girl. No need to be rude to me."

Grace hated the direction their exchange was heading and wished she had turned back when she'd had the chance.

"You should be friendlier to your neighbours. Come on, Simba." He yanked at the dog's lead and barged past Grace.

She shivered, disgusted by his touch, and crossed the road towards her house.

"The walk of shame at thirty-one, Grace. Really? I can't believe you sometimes." Valerie didn't wait until she was in the door to start the attack.

She grimaced. "I'm not in the mood, Mum. I've already had a run-in with old man Wilson across the road."

"Don't you think I worry about you? Out of respect for me, you could have let me know you were staying out for the night. There are young girls being murdered out there." Valerie glared at her daughter, obviously waiting for a response.

Grace returned the silent stare for a few moments, her hangover enticing no interest in her mother's words. Valerie raised her eyebrows, and she knew the lecture was imminent. She curled her upper lip and inched her face closer to her mother's.

"Shut up!" she roared. Grace whirled round, her long black coat following with such speed, it lashed against Valerie's legs. She yanked open the front door, and it ricocheted off the wall while she stormed back out onto the street.

By the time Grace arrived at the cemetery, heavy tears were falling down her face. She sat against her grandfather's temporary headstone, put there solely to distinguish who was buried under the mound of earth. In a few months, the black granite memorial stone would be erected, and Grace and Valerie had agreed it would be a special place they could visit together. At the moment, she sat alone on the cold muddy ground, bare of grass. With her knees bent and drawn in close to her body, she rested her chin and let the tears stain her cheeks.

"I don't know what's happened to me, Granddad. I feel so emotional all the time. I really thought returning to work would help; keeping busy with people constantly around was a great distraction. But sometimes it's more frustrating because I feel like I'm constantly putting a face on. Just plodding along, doing what's expected of me, and smiling at the right time. But deep down, I'm angry and sad and I miss you."

Her sobs quickly became uncontrollable. Tears mixed with snot as she sank further into her grief. The breeze circled and howled through the swaying trees. She mirrored Mother Nature's wail, using her sleeve to wipe her sodden face.

"And the way I'm speaking to Mum! You would go ballistic if you were here. I know they say you take your pain and frustration out on those closest to you, but I have to remember she's lost her dad. She's dealt with the past few months so well, been so strong. And here I am, acting like a fucked-up freak. We had time to say goodbye to you. We knew the cancer would take you, so I can't understand why I'm so emotional all the time. I'll have to apologise to her. She's more than my mum. She's my best friend, and we don't speak to each other like this."

Grace slammed the ground in frustration. The tears had dried from her puffy eyes, and she vacantly looked out across the cemetery for another half hour before moving. She wiped her swollen cheeks aggressively and filled her lungs with a deep breath. "I have to pull myself together. I can't keep blaming your death for my emotions."

She got to her feet, rubbed her bum to regain some feeling there, and placed her hand on the headstone. "Guide me if you can, Granddad. I need to get back to my normal self."

Grace walked leisurely back to the cemetery entrance, welcoming the coolness against her burning face. When she reached the gate, just before the main road, a beautiful white butterfly flew around her head for a moment before soaring into the sky out of sight.

She smiled. "Thanks for listening, Granddad."

CHAPTER FIFTEEN

Hamilton crouched over the dead body.

"This attack was definitely more aggressive, Inspector," Laura said during her preliminary findings. "The knife wounds would lead me to suggest we're dealing with the same killer, but there are some obvious differences with this victim."

He closed his eyes and sighed, devastated that another woman had been brutally murdered on his patch. "Yes, it is obvious, Laura. This amount of blood indicates his violence has significantly escalated. She suffered a worse torture. We assumed the last murder was personal, but that seems nothing compared to this one. Interestingly, he's chosen a blonde lady this time."

Clarke joined them and winced as he examined the victim. "Jesus, this one took a bloody beating."

Laura's mouth set in a hard line, and Hamilton cringed at his partner's unprofessionalism. He thought it best they leave the pathology team to get on with their work as soon as possible.

"Boss, I've got the victim's identification from her purse. It was left behind again," Clarke said.

"Lewis, just go and get the motor started. I'll meet you out there. Laura, it's imperative I get the post-mortem information as soon as possible, so I'm going to send DS Morris and Wedlock over to the mortuary to be present. If that's okay with you?"

"No problem at all, Inspector. My team and I have some more work to do here. We need to thoroughly check the scene for DNA before we pack up. Send them to the mortuary in about two hours. I should be ready for them then." Laura returned to preparing a body bag for the fourth victim.

Hamilton marched to the car and jumped in. "That was not acceptable, Lewis. Be careful how you speak about the victims when it's not just my company you're in."

Clarke frowned, and Hamilton hoped he wasn't considering a sarcastic retort. He raised his own eyebrows to warn his partner of his foul mood and was satisfied when Clarke nodded without saying a word. The journey to the station was driven in complete silence; not even the radio played. Clarke was sulking for being reprimanded, but he understood his partner needed time to mope before shrugging it off and returning to his jovial self.

When they reached the incident room, he called for the attention of his team while Clarke updated the information on the board.

"Okay, listen up." Hamilton cleared his throat. "Our victim is Emily Donovan, twenty-five years old, so our youngest victim. She lived with her parents in Shepherd's Bush. Kerry, I want you to go with Lewis and inform the family."

"But, sir, I've never done that before," Fraser interrupted him.

"We all have to start somewhere, sergeant," he snapped and instantly regretted it as the colour rose in her cheeks. "Look, Kerry, I know this is something I usually handle, but I have a meeting with DCI Allen that, annoyingly, I can't get out of. Lewis has done this plenty of times, so use this as an experience to learn and just follow his lead."

"Stick with me, kid. I'll show you the ropes," Clarke joked, but the perplexed expression on Fraser's face showed her anxiety.

"Ask the parents if Emily had any boyfriends and who she was out with last night. It might help us with a lead. Because if we thought the last attack was personal, this one just upped the stakes." Hamilton continued to explain the differences in the latest murder and informed Morris and Wedlock that their next duty was to attend the post-mortem. "I can't stress enough how much we need a break in this case. DCI Allen won't let me reschedule this meeting because he wants a full update, and I'm furious that I have to tell him we've found another body." He punched the desk he was sitting on.

"Hey, boss. Look at this," Clarke called from the information board. "Michelle, our first victim, was a stage actress in Central London, and Emily worked as a runner in a theatre. Albeit two different theatres, they're both in close proximity."

Hamilton stood next to his partner, crossed his arms, and glared at the board with him, searching for more clues.

"Sir, *The Lady in Red* was the name of a theatre show in London," Fraser added.

Hamilton snapped round to face her.

"I only know because my mum had tickets and said the opening had been postponed after the newspaper articles. Gosh, I'm so sorry I didn't connect the dots before."

"Okay, Kerry, don't beat yourself up about it. The main thing is we have a connection now. Let's find out what we can about these theatres, and the one that postponed their show."

"It was The London, sir. Where Emily worked." Fraser hung her head.

"What?" Hamilton exclaimed. "Hold your head up, and less of the dramatics. Sometimes it just takes one of us to look at the information and pull the clues from it, so well done, to all of you. Remember, we're a team, and we wouldn't have had these added bits of information so quickly without you, Kerry."

He was buzzing inside, feeling excited for the first time since the case opened at the beginning of December. Finally, they had a possible connection between two of their victims. His heart raced. "This could be what we've been looking for, guys. I'm eager to get on with investigating this clue, but I'm all too aware that we have meetings to adhere to. Let's get those tasks done and dusted and meet back here in an hour, if that's possible." He addressed Morris and Wedlock with the last point, unsure how long their task might take.

"I want the first team back in the office to start digging into these theatres. See if there's any overlap in employees; concentrate on men that may have been dismissed in the last six months, anything that stands out. Also check out our second victim, Kate, again. She worked in a doctor's surgery, but let's not discount that she may have worked in one of these theatres at some point."

"Boss, it was yet another anonymous tip alerting us to this victim," Wedlock said as he put on his coat.

"Yes, let's not forget that," Clarke replied. "But every time we've delved into those calls, they've been dead ends. They were made from local phone boxes with no street cameras observing them."

Hamilton interrupted. "Let's not disregard it, add it to the board. From now on, I don't want us to overlook any piece of information. The slightest thing we think of, uncover, or are troubled by, I want you speak up immediately. Right, meet you all back here."

He watched proudly as his team left the incident room. Because of their enthusiastic chatter, he knew they felt the same spark of excitement about the case. He climbed the stairs to DCI Allen's office, clinging to that sentiment as he prepared himself for the interrogation coming his way.

CHAPTER SIXTEEN

Once home from the cemetery, Grace ate, showered, and began to feel human again as the hangover finally wore off. Valerie had ignored her all evening, highlighting her furious mood. Her mother always forgave friends' and family's transgressions easily, too easily, she believed, so this behaviour towards Grace forced her to make the first move in an effort to restore their relationship.

While her mother sat comfortably in the living room reading a book, Grace slipped into the kitchen and made them both a cup of tea. She hoped the awkward atmosphere would vanish once she explained how awful she felt. Pausing at the doorway for a moment, she watched Valerie; her legs curled up on the brown, faux leather two-seater sofa, sandy-coloured hair twisted in a clip, as always to keep it off her face. Her blue eyes shone in comparison to her dull, tired-looking face. Guilt struck hard in Grace's stomach when she thought of how she had spoken to her mother, a selfless woman who always gave to people and never took.

She inhaled a deep breath and walked in. "Here, Mum. I thought you might like a cup of tea."

Valerie remained quiet as she closed her book, placed it on the coffee table, and accepted the warm drink from her daughter.

Grace hated the unnatural tension between them; it was suffocating her. But she was well aware she had created it herself. "I'm really sorry for how I spoke to you earlier," she said quietly.

Valerie just sipped her tea and barely looked in her direction.

"I know I haven't been my usual self since Granddad died, and I'm sorry. I feel okay at work; I mean I can at least get through the day without becoming an emotional tornado. But then, sometimes, I just feel a bit lost. Plus, I'm not sleeping very well," she blurted out, trying to find an excuse for her constant mood swings.

Valerie placed her cup on the table and gently held her daughter's free hand. Grace felt instantly comforted by her mother's touch. "I know it's hard for you, Grace. I lost him too. But I do feel like I'm walking on eggshells around you most of the time, worried that if I say the wrong thing, we'll be thrown into yet another argument. Or worse, you'll storm out of the house and I have no idea where you are for hours."

"I'm sorry."

"I'm not looking for an apology, my darling. I only want to help you."

"It's just something I have to get through, Mum. Everyone grieves in their own way, right?"

Still holding Grace's hand, Valerie moved closer to her. "It's okay to accept help, love. Or at least to talk about how you're feeling. Yes, everyone grieves differently, but I don't think bottling it up inside is going to help you. Oh, darling! I'm just so worried about you. I don't know what to do for the best. Your constant lack of respect for me, the mood swings, and binge drinking."

Grace could see it pained her mother to be so honest with her. She wanted to weep herself when a single teardrop fell from Valerie's eye. She placed her own cup on the table, let go of her mother's hand, and embraced her tightly. She knew it was time to be honest with her mother and herself.

"Mum. I'm having these really awful dreams."

The pair pulled apart, and they both wiped away their tears.

"What, you mean like nightmares?" Valerie asked.

"Well, yes. They are scary and dark, but I can't always remember them," she explained.

"Hang on, I don't understand. How can they be so awful if you can't remember them?"

"That's the thing, Mum. Sometimes I can only remember how they made me feel. Then there are other times when I first wake up and I see flashes of images, but mostly they just make me panic. It's like I'm being haunted in my sleep."

"And what are these images you're seeing?"

"A dead body." Grace covered her eyes. "What do you think that means? Why am I dreaming of things like that?"

"I don't know, sweetheart. But you have to remember you are dealing with a lot of death at the moment. Seeing Granddad laid out at the funeral parlour may not have been the best thing for you. Perhaps it's affecting you now."

"Really? You think so?"

Valerie sighed. "This is what I meant about dealing with everything alone. Your emotions are eating away at you and seeping into your unconscious. A factor, I would say, that's influencing your sleeping patterns and moods."

She began to feel calmer as she listened to her mother's logical explanation.

Valerie reached for her handbag by the side of the sofa and rooted through it, pulling out a business card and handing it to Grace. "Now I know I made the right decision getting this for you. I'm so glad you've opened up to me, sweetheart, but I really think you would benefit from bereavement counselling. Please, I'm begging you to consider it."

Grace cautiously took the card from her mother's hand, already guessing what was printed on it. She peered down at the plain white card with its simple black lettering: *Maria Lee, Psychiatrist & Clinical Hypnotherapist.*

CHAPTER SEVENTEEN

The incident room was a hive of activity when Morris and Wedlock returned from the post-mortem. Hamilton rushed from his office to greet them, and the rest of the team stopped what they were doing to listen to the update.

"Finally!" Hamilton said as he reached for his coat. "We're on our way to interview Emily Donovan's colleagues, but I wanted to see you first. What took so long?"

"Sorry, gov. There was a hold-up at the mortuary. Nothing we could do," Wedlock explained. "Laura should have sent the full report while we were driving back here. It pains me to say this, but there's still no damn DNA."

Hamilton could relate to his sergeant's exasperated expression while delivering the news. He wracked his brain: *could the killer really be so meticulous that he never leaves a shred of evidence?*

"Sir?" Morris jolted him from his thoughts. "In short, the head injuries knocked our victim unconscious, and their brutality may have led to her death if she was left there. But it was the intensive stab wounds directly through the heart that killed her."

"Thanks, you two," Hamilton said after a long sigh. "Come on, Lewis! Let's get to this theatre and see what we can uncover there."

"Sir, did the family add anything of significance?" Wedlock called out as the two detectives headed out of the room.

"Catch up with Kerry. She'll fill you in," he shouted back as the door closed behind him.

Once they were downstairs, Hamilton jumped into the driver's seat of his silver Vauxhall Corsa, and Clarke took the passenger's seat to enter their location into the sat nav—automatic actions of partners who understood their roles. Chit-chat was kept to a minimum during the journey as they both contemplated the case and where it was headed.

****

Hamilton stood tall on the stage of The London theatre, staring out at the empty rows of seats. He'd never understood the need for fame and fortune. Personally, he looked forward to a hot cup of coffee while curled up with his wife, watching a series on Netflix.

"Wouldn't it be amazing to have all those seats filled, all their attention on you?" Clarke interrupted Hamilton's peaceful thoughts. "Not unless a murderer was out there watching you, of course."

A man in his late forties, with a comb-over of thinning dark hair and dressed in a burgundy suit with gold buttons fastening it, approached the stage. Hamilton couldn't help but notice, and dislike, the eccentric swirls and colourful patterns of the man's tie.

"I'm so sorry to have kept you waiting. I'm Michael Sparks, director of the theatre." Michael outstretched his hand.

"I'm Detective Inspector Denis Hamilton, and this is Detective Sergeant Lewis Clarke," he said, as he let go of Michael's hand and pulled his warrant card from his inside pocket. "Is there somewhere more private we can talk?"

"Of course. Follow me, please."

As Michael led them through the narrow corridor, a young brunette lady appeared out of a side office. She was petite and slim. Her small features highlighted her natural beauty, flawless porcelain skin, and warm brown eyes.

"This is Assistant Director Grace Murphy. Will you need to talk with her too, or was it just me you wanted?" Michael asked.

"Please join us, Ms. Murphy. Your input could be helpful." Hamilton waited until the two turned their backs on him and continued walking, then he quickly peeped at Clarke, who acknowledged him with a slight nod.

They squeezed into Michael's office, which was more like a small box bedroom than a director's office. Hamilton observed Michael and Grace's interaction with interest; they never spoke, and the man took his seat behind the desk, motioning for his deputy to stand next to him. Michael then gestured for Hamilton to take the seat opposite him, but he ignored the offer.

"I must say, I find it strange no one has thought to ask why we're here." Hamilton frowned. "So I'll just get straight to the point. We're investigating the murder of Emily Donovan, and we believe she worked here."

"What?" Grace screeched. "When? How?"

"Yes, I thought that was why you were here," Michael said.

Grace's attention snapped back to her boss. "What? How do you already know?"

"Sorry, I've not been long off the phone with her sister, Hayley. I was coming to tell you when I received a message that the detectives were waiting for me out front."

"What happened to her, Detective?" Grace asked, turning pale.

"I hope you can appreciate I can't share all the information with you at this point in the investigation," Hamilton said. "But it happened on Friday night, Ms. Murphy. Now, Emily worked here as the theatre's runner. Is that correct?"

"Yes," Michael replied, standing to offer the woman his seat.

"Did she have any relationships with anyone at work? Was there anyone you can think of that she didn't get along with?" Hamilton asked.

Though frustrated that no one asked him, he waited for Michael to pour Grace a glass of water from the jug on his table. He could see the young lady was in shock. Her eyes were wide, and she was struggling for air.

"Ms. Murphy, are you okay?" he asked.

"Yes. Well, no. Obviously, I can't believe it... how can she have been murdered?"

"I'm afraid *we* have to ask these questions."

"Of course, Inspector," Michael said. "And yes, Emily was having a fling with Eric. Caught them a couple of times at it in my theatre!"

Grace's head shot up, and she stared at Michael again, but he continued to talk without looking at her.

"Of course, we can't condone that kind of unprofessional behaviour, and I explained to Emily that she was on her last warning."

"And Eric would be…?" Hamilton asked, while Clarke jotted notes in his pad.

"Our lead actor, Eric Dexter," Grace whispered.

"Could we speak with Mr. Dexter?"

"Not here, you can't. He called in sick this morning. Annoying really, as now I'll have to check the understudy is up to scratch."

"He called in sick?" Grace asked.

Michael continued to address Hamilton. "Yes. He called in just before you two arrived, immediately after I ended the call with Hayley."

"Right. Well, we'll need his address then please, Mr. Sparks," Hamilton explained.

Michael crossed the small room and searched through a row of folders on the shelf. He opened one, took out a sheet of paper, and handed it to Clarke, who copied the address and handed it back.

Hamilton had one more question he needed to ask before leaving. "Do you know if Emily left work with anyone last Friday night?"

"We were the last ones out of the theatre on Friday," Grace answered.

"Yes. Emily, Eric, and I left at the same time, a few minutes after Grace. Emily said she was meeting some friends for a drink and walked off towards Leicester Square. Eric and I parted at the Underground," Michael informed them.

"Okay, well, it seems we should have a chat with Mr. Dexter," Hamilton said. "Thank you for your time, Mr. Sparks, Ms.

Murphy. If we have any other questions, we'll be in touch. And if you think of anything that might be of interest to the case, please call me." He slid his business card onto the table.

As they turned to leave the office, Clarke peered over his shoulder. "Didn't you have a play called *The Lady in Red* that was due to start last month?"

Michael curled his lips. A menacing look spread over his face, but only for a few seconds. He quickly regained his poise. "Yes, we did. But after the press gave one of the murder victims that very same name, we didn't think it was great publicity. We've rejigged a few things, and thankfully, we'll be ready to throw the curtains up in February. Tickets are still available if you fancy it, gentlemen."

****

After the detectives had closed the door behind them, Grace rested her head on the table and sobbed. She felt Michael's arm slide around her shoulders. Though the kind gesture was meant to console her, something about his embrace made her feel uneasy. She stood up and walked round the desk to put some space between herself and her boss. She wiped her eyes, a headache brewing. It was descending on her fast, as though she'd been knocked with a sledgehammer.

"I just cannot believe this has happened, Michael. Someone we worked with has been murdered. This is terrible." Fresh tears sprang to her eyes, but she wiped those away too and tried to control her emotions.

"I know, my dear, one of ours being murdered like that. It doesn't bear thinking about." He moved forward as if to touch Grace's arm, but she walked farther away and stood by the door.

"We'll have to call a meeting, Michael. The rest of the crew should hear the news from us. My God, do you think they already know? Found out while we were in here with the police? If Hayley is ringing people to inform them, it's probably all over Facebook too. You know how this kind of news spreads. The team will be emotional wrecks." The tears finally escaped from her eyes once again.

"Calm down, Grace. I think *you're* the emotional wreck at the moment. We'll need to be the strong ones. That's not just our team out there; they are our employees. They'll be looking to us for support and guidance. We cannot show them *that*," Michael said, pointing at the mascara streaks staining her face.

"Yes, okay," she agreed but felt hurt by his harsh attitude. She understood that some people could keep a barrier up against their emotions, but this situation was different. *How can he be so unmoved about what has happened? Emily is dead.*

"Now, go and freshen up, Grace. Make yourself look beautiful again. Your eyes look a bit red and puffy. We'll regroup back here in twenty minutes and face the crew together."

Once she was in the safety of her office, Grace gulped air as though she'd been holding her breath underwater. She slid to the ground, her back against the door. She tentatively slipped her hands into her cardigan pocket. The business card felt like a scorching object, demanding her to make a choice. She pulled it out and read the details over and over for a few moments. *I think it's time I called this shrink.*

****

Hamilton and Clarke parked outside a row of terraced apartments in Maida Vale. They all looked pristine with freshly painted front doors and neatly trimmed pot plants decorating the front steps.

"I couldn't live here. Everything looks the same; it's a bit creepy, really. Like a cult," Clarke grumbled, as they climbed the stairs to the front door.

"You couldn't live here because you can't afford it, Lewis." Hamilton smirked as he lifted the brass handle and knocked on the shiny black door. "I'll take the lead with the questions."

"As always, boss."

A slender, tanned man answered the door, wearing grey jogging bottoms and a black T-shirt. His eyes were swollen, and there were balled-up tissues in his hand.

"Mr. Eric Dexter?" Hamilton asked.

"Yes, that's me," the man sniffled in reply.

"I'm Detective Inspector Denis Hamilton, and this is Detective Sergeant Lewis Clarke."

They flipped out their warrant cards in unison.

"All right if we come in and ask you a few questions."

Eric turned and led them into the front lounge. A cream three-piece suite surrounded by chrome-and-mirror-effect furniture greeted them. Two bookshelves were decorated with photos of Eric and various people in glitzy outfits at parties.

"Other wannabe celebrities, I bet," Clarke whispered.

Hamilton raised his eyebrows at his partner. They both ogled a huge canvas hung on the wall; nine images of Eric's face in different bright colours stared back at them.

"It's pop art," Eric explained.

Hamilton held in a chuckle as his partner smiled and nodded in mock interest. They both took a seat on the sofa, and Eric followed suit, sitting in the leather armchair by the window.

"I assume you're here about Emily."

"Yes, Mr. Dexter, we are. We visited The London Theatre this morning, and Mr. Sparks informed us that you called in sick today," Hamilton replied.

"Can you blame me? I'm in shock. I wouldn't be able to give my best performance. Not even in rehearsals."

"So you and Miss Donovan were dating?" Hamilton asked, and Eric's hesitation made him curious. "Mr. Dexter?"

"Well, it's complicated. Yes, we dated, but nothing was *official*. We've been on and off for a while now."

"How did you find out Emily had been murdered?"

"Hayley, her sister, rang me after the family found out. She knew that we had a bit of a thing going on, and thankfully, she thought I should hear it from her and not the newspaper," Eric replied as he used the balled-up tissue to wipe his eyes.

"When did you last see Emily?" Hamilton continued to fire questions at the man, eager to see if he would hesitate again.

"Friday. We left the theatre together, but she went to meet some friends at a local bar, and I caught the tube home alone. I didn't see her after that." Eric lowered his head into his hands.

"Did that bother you, Mr. Dexter? That she had plans that didn't include you?"

"No! Why would you think that?"

Hamilton ignored the question. "Where were you during the early hours of Saturday morning, let's say between three and six a.m.?"

Eric drew in a deep breath. "I was here, at home, all night. And have been since."

"Can anyone confirm that?"

Hamilton's interest was piqued further as Eric shifted in his seat and remained quiet.

"Can anyone confirm that you were at home the night Emily Donovan was murdered?" Hamilton repeated with more urgency.

"Maybe. Well, yes, actually, because I wasn't alone. But obviously it wasn't Emily, so I'd rather not divulge that information."

"Mr. Dexter, we are in the middle of a murder investigation, and our latest victim is the woman you were having a relationship with. You will divulge that information with us right now if you want to be eliminated from our enquiries."

"Are you suggesting that I had something to do with this?" Eric's voice rose, and he stood up. "How dare you—"

"It would be wise if you calmed down." Hamilton moved to the edge of his seat, prepared to restrain the man if he had to.

Clarke mirrored his action.

"We're not suggesting anything at this time, but surely you understand why we need to clarify your alibi."

Eric nodded and sat down again. "Of course. I'm sorry. It's just not a great position I find myself in right now. You must understand Emily and I were not exclusive. I'm sure she was seeing other men too."

"Mr. Dexter?" Hamilton said, his patience dwindling.

"I was with Grace. She works at the theatre with me. Actually, she's my boss, the assistant director. It's all rather embarrassing."

"Grace Murphy?" Clarke confirmed as he flipped back through his notes.

"Yes. I bumped into her Friday evening, hours after we'd left the theatre. She had been in the pub with friends. We ran into each other after she had left and came back here for a few more. One thing led to another, and she stayed the night. It was silly, really. I think we both knew it shouldn't have happened and that's why she scarpered the next morning while I was in the shower."

"Thank you, Mr. Dexter," Hamilton said. "Obviously, we'll have to meet with Ms. Murphy again to corroborate your alibi. Here's my card. If you can think of anything else we should know about, give me a call. We'll see ourselves out."

Safe in the privacy of the car, the detectives spoke freely with each other. "Strange Grace Murphy didn't offer us that bit of information this morning," Clarke said, double-checking his notes from earlier.

"Yes, I know why you're thinking that, Lewis, but she was in a terrible state of shock."

"Seems quite a bit of extracurricular activities take place at The London Theatre."

Hamilton snorted. "I've noticed! But I don't know… there's something about that guy I do not like. I just don't know what it is exactly."

He drummed his fingers on the steering wheel as he drove. "Right, back to the station so I can check in with the team. While we're there, we can get Ms. Murphy's home address and pay her a visit later on, see if she backs up Mr. Dexter's story."

CHAPTER EIGHTEEN

The shadowy evening crept through the window, causing silhouettes to dance on Grace's bedroom wall. She switched on her desk lamp to brighten the room, wrapped her woolly cardigan tighter around her and scrolled through Facebook on the laptop. She peered at Michelle's and Kate's accounts and took another swig of wine. After scrolling through photographs from their parties and celebrations, she read updates about promotions, new partners, and praise for performances or sober days. *I feel awful that I didn't stay in touch with you both. And now I'll never have the chance to.* Grace gulped another mouthful of her drink then clicked the defriend button, first on Michelle's account then Kate's. She was saddened by the thought of never reading any virtual updates from them again. *I can't believe you're both gone. Murdered. This world has become a scary and violent place to live in.* A knock at the door interrupted Grace's thoughts.

"Honey, two policemen are here to see you," Valerie said as she peered into the room. "They're waiting in the living room."

"Oh, okay, thanks, Mum. I'm coming."

Grace quickly followed her mother downstairs. When she entered the room, she saw the two detectives she'd met earlier already sitting comfortable on the sofa.

"Ms. Murphy, I hope you don't mind us coming to see you again, but we'd like to ask you a few more questions." Hamilton stood and shook her hand.

"Please, call me Grace. It's no problem. Of course, ask your questions," she replied.

"Okay, Grace." Hamilton smiled at her briefly. "We spoke with Mr. Dexter this afternoon, and he led us to believe that the two of you were together last Friday night. Is that true?"

Her cheeks burned instantly and she turned to check Valerie wasn't standing in the doorway. Satisfied her mother wasn't eavesdropping, she met Hamilton's gaze. "Yes, unfortunately, it is true. It wasn't very professional of me at all."

"I must admit we were surprised you didn't think this was important enough to mention this morning. Especially as we explained we would pay him a visit."

"I was deeply shocked by the news of Emily's death, Inspector. I wasn't thinking straight, but I didn't really think you would need an alibi for Eric. Plus, it's really not information I would want my boss to find out, but I apologise." Grace finally raised her eyes to meet Hamilton's.

"What time did you meet up with Mr. Dexter on Friday evening?"

"Well, I didn't meet up with him exactly. I literally ran right into him on the street." Grace recalled to the two detectives what happened the night she met Eric.

"And what time did you leave the next morning?"

"Erm… it was seven thirty when I left his apartment. I checked my phone. After I woke up, Eric came into the bedroom, and we spoke for a few minutes. Thankfully, he went straight into the en-suite for a shower, and I used the opportunity to get out as fast as I could. I'm embarrassed about the whole situation."

"Where had Mr. Dexter come from?"

Grace frowned. "I don't understand. What do you mean?"

"Well you didn't wake up together, you just said. So where was Mr. Dexter?"

"Oh, I don't know. The kitchen, maybe. He was in his boxer shorts!"

"But he left the room without you noticing?"

"Erm… I'm not entirely sure how the evening went. Too much alcohol. We were definitely still in his lounge at midnight, because the friend I had been with that night rang me, and I let it go to voicemail. We made a sick joke about letting her worry." Grace looked away again, ashamed of her actions.

"But after midnight, the details become hazy, and you woke alone in his bed, yes?" Hamilton smiled but held up his hand, preventing her from answering. "Grace, as you've probably read in the tabloids by now, there are another three victims involved in this investigation, Michelle Young, Kate Wakeman and Vicky Lawlor."

"Yes, I know, and it pains me to say I knew Michelle and Kate." Her trepidation grew at the thought of the vindictive people roaming free, but she didn't want to crumble in front of the detectives.

"We discovered you were mutual friends on Facebook, but could you tell us how you knew the women?" Hamilton continued.

Grace studied his face. The warmth in his brown eyes, his smooth caramel skin, and his genuine smile drew her in. She stopped fumbling with her fingers and took a deep breath.

"Although we were friends on Facebook, I actually hadn't spoken to them in years. I went to the same secondary school as Michelle. We were friendly enough but didn't have a lasting relationship. I haven't seen her since we left sixth form college. Kate and I used to drink in the same pub, and we were good friends for a few years, but then you get caught up in life. I went off to university, and last I heard, she had given up the booze, so we never bumped into each other. So it must be at least seven years since I've seen her. Gosh, that's a long time. Detective, I'm so sorry. Should I have mentioned this to you earlier?" Grace's eyes welled up, but she quickly brushed them away.

"Of course not, you couldn't have known there was a connection in the murders. We're just ensuring that we follow up every possible association in the cases," Hamilton continued. "Did you know Mr. Dexter and Miss Donovan were dating?"

"Not really. It came as quite a surprise to me. Eric and I had gone for a drink after work one night, and he briefly spoke of someone he was seeing, but he didn't mention Emily's name. I honestly feel so foolish about spending that Friday night with him. I wish I could erase it from my memory. If only life were that simple. He told me about a woman who had cheated on him, then I saw him having sex with Emily at the theatre, and that same night, I stayed at his apartment. I should have known he was just another ladies' man."

Hamilton nodded while his partner scribbled down everything Grace shared with them. "Just one final question before we leave, Grace. Do you know how Mr. Dexter and Kate Wakeman knew each other?"

"I didn't know they did. Wait! Are you telling me that Kate was another conquest of Eric's? I feel even more of an idiot now." Grace frowned. "Hang on a minute, Inspector. Could Eric be involved in all this?"

"I'm not saying anything of the sort. It was a simple question to gauge the connections between our victims. Obviously, you can understand that to find a link in a case like this can be of the utmost importance." Hamilton stood up to leave. "I'll leave you my card, and if you think of anything, then please do let me know straight away this time."

Grace felt slightly reprimanded, but took the card and escorted the detectives to the front door.

"One last thing. Please be extra vigilant when you're out and about. This is the fourth murder investigation we're looking into, all young women in your age group. So spread the word amongst your friends and make sure you don't travel alone late at night."

"Of course, Inspector. Thank you. It's so scary to think these awful crimes are happening where I live and work. To people that I know," Grace said, opening the door.

Hamilton and Clarke stepped onto the front porch.

"We'll be releasing a statement to the media shortly, but please remember what I said about being alert at all times," Hamilton repeated.

"Thank you," she replied.

"Nice to see you have the neighbourhood watch on your doorstep," Clarke added.

Grace followed the man's gaze to Mr. Wilson's house across the street and just caught sight of a twitching net curtain.

"I'm afraid it's more inappropriate nosey neighbours with that one, Detective."

CHAPTER NINETEEN

When Grace arrived at work the following morning, she rushed to her office, not wanting to put off the task any longer. Although she usually felt empowered and businesslike at her desk, she trembled as she lifted the phone from its dock station. Right at that moment, the nerves took hold. Her mouth dried up, and she wondered if she would be able to string a sentence together. But before she had the chance to talk herself out of the task, she dialled the number on the business card.

"Hello, Maria Lee speaking. How may I help?"

"Oh. Hello. Hi. Yes, I think I need some help. Make an appointment for some counselling, maybe, I mean." Grace heard a small giggle down the phone line and cringed at herself. "I'm sorry. Let me start again. My name is Grace Murphy, and my mum gave me your business card. She suggested I give you a call."

"Please don't apologise, dear. It can be a very daunting experience for some people to make this type of call," Maria said, and Grace could hear the warmth in the lady's voice.

"You've tackled the first stumbling block just by talking to me. How do you think I can help you, Grace?"

"Oh. Erm… I'm not really sure. I'm sorry, you're right; this is difficult. Maybe I'm not ready."

"Don't give up so quickly. Why don't you tell me why your mother gave you my details and suggested you call me?"

"My grandfather passed away."

"I am sorry, Grace. My condolences."

"Thank you. The thing is, if I'm honest with myself, I haven't been coping too well. My moods are up and down like a yo-yo, especially towards my mum, who I suppose is getting the brunt of it. I'm having trouble sleeping. I feel really anxious and can't switch off—unless I have a drink, then I fall into a deep sleep. But I'm also having nightmares, when I do manage to sleep, that is." Grace stopped to catch her breath.

"It sounds to me like you have a lot on your mind, dear. I would be happy to explore this further with you. Let me look at the diary to see when we can book you an appointment. It's difficult to explain your feelings over the phone."

The line went quiet for a few moments, and Grace was very aware of how fast her heart was pounding. She gripped the phone in an attempt to stop the trembling. *I can't believe how nervous I am.*

"Grace, sorry to keep you waiting. How does Friday evening suit you? Let's say five p.m.?" Maria finally said.

"Oh wow! That is quick. I thought I'd be on a waiting list for a few weeks."

"Please don't feel anxious, Grace. I work from a small office above my home, so it's very informal. I prefer this method, as I think it's a calm environment. I don't have an enormous list of patients as I work alone and like to give an intimate one-to-one service. I want to build a relationship with you. You've made the decision to choose me, so as my patient, I'd like to show you that same consideration by giving you my full attention."

"I see. I guess I'm not really sure how it all works. Or really how you can help. I mean, it's just grief and lack of sleep. I'd hate to waste your time." Grace backtracked, offended at being referred to as a patient.

"The first appointment is tailored exactly for that. It gives us a chance to meet each other and decide whether or not this is the right thing. For both of us. Let's give it a go on Friday, and you can decide after that. As I said, it's a very informal chat. Please don't worry about it. Get a pen, and I'll give you my address."

Grace scribbled the psychiatrist's address on her notepad and ended the call. She contemplated her writing and daydreamed, completely unaware she wasn't alone any more.

"Penny for them."

Grace jumped, startled by the voice. She looked up from the notepad and saw Michael leaning against the doorframe, staring at her.

"Fuck! You scared me. How long have you been standing there? I thought I shut the door!" Grace ripped off the piece of paper and slipped it into her pocket.

Michael's eyes widened. "I did knock. There's no need to be rude."

"I'm not being rude. I just don't like people creeping up on me. I said, how long have you been standing there?"

"Well, not long. You must have been on the phone when I knocked. I opened the door, and you were staring off into space. You looked very pretty. But then, you always do, of course." He smiled.

"Don't give me that bullshit. It's polite to wait until the person says 'come in,'" Grace growled.

The pair glared at each other for a few seconds. "I hate to remind you, Grace, but I am actually your superior. *I* am the director of this theatre, not you. Yes, I let you have the upper hand around here mostly, because I respect you. You're a talented lady. But I think you should show me that same respect. I do not appreciate being spoken to like this."

"It's been a stressful few months."

Michael continued to scowl at her, and Grace knew he expected an apology. *Keep waiting, mate.*

He took a deep breath and exhaled slowly. "Fine, if that's how you want to play it, Grace. I just came to tell you that Eric has called in sick again today. Can you believe that? Doesn't he care what this means for us? He's the star of the show. We've already had one setback! This is all we need."

"Michael! He's grieving. Do you have no compassion? Plus, that's what we have understudies for," Grace replied sarcastically.

"Ha! Grieving! They were shagging each other, not engaged. He probably sleeps with every woman he meets." Michael paused, and the tension intensified. "Except you, of course. You've got class, right?" He moved closer and leaned his hands on the desk. His face edged nearer to hers.

A rush of heat scorched her cheeks, and she cursed herself for relenting, giving Michael the reaction he desired. *Shit! No, he can't know what happened between me and Eric… can he?* She stood up from the desk, and he copied her actions, their eyes locked on one another's.

"All that attention is part and parcel of being the star of all the shows, I guess," Grace mumbled ignoring the personal comment.

"Well, he'll be no star of this show if he continues to call in *sick*," Michael mocked. "I've been watching his understudy, Blake, with some interest, and I like what I see from him. Maybe he'll be the lead in my new show. I don't want the risk of any more controversial press with this one, either."

Grace headed for the office door. "Let's not worry then. If you say Blake is showing promise, I'm sure it'll be a success. Shall we get the morning meeting started?"

"Of course it will be a success, Grace. We're working together." Michael smirked as Grace turned and walked away.

CHAPTER TWENTY

The two detectives sat in the same position they had the previous day in Eric's lounge, and Hamilton scanned the room. He spotted two wine glasses on the corner unit, and Eric was dressed in the same outfit as he wore when they'd first met him.

"Mr. Dexter, we wanted to let you know that Ms. Murphy corroborated your alibi for the night Emily Donovan was murdered."

Eric cringed, no doubt at his cold and informative tone.

"We're just unsure as to why you didn't mention Kate Wakeman?"

"What? Who the hell is Kate Wakeman?"

"She was recently murdered, Mr. Dexter. It would appear that the two of you were also friends, and you neglected to share that information with us."

"What! No, we weren't. I've never met anyone called Kate Wakeman."

"Not according to Facebook."

"Facebook?" Eric's eyes darted back and forth between the detectives, then he frowned. "I don't know half the people on my Facebook page."

Hamilton sighed. "Care to elaborate, Mr. Dexter?"

"I'm a stage actor, Inspector. I regularly get Facebook friend requests after a show. I like the attention from my fans, so I accept them. It doesn't mean I've met them. Or that we're friends. Or that I even bloody know them, for that matter. To be honest, I hardly reply to any of their messages. Have a look through my account. You're welcome to my password. You won't find much interaction with my fans."

"We will be looking at everything in detail, thank you. Did you have company last night, Mr. Dexter?" Hamilton asked, nodding in the direction of the wine glasses.

"I don't really think that's any of your business. But as I have nothing to hide, I'll tell you. Hayley came over. I think we both needed a shoulder to cry on."

"Emily Donovan's sister?"

"Yes," Eric replied. "But nothing happened! We had a few glasses of wine, shared our memories of Emily, and she left. Honest!"

"Don't feel like you have to convince us. The grieving period is a difficult one, even more so in circumstances like these. Just one last question before we leave, Mr. Dexter: do you know a young lady called Vicky Lawlor?"

Eric paused for a moment. "No."

"Okay, well, thank you for your time. We'll be in touch if we need any further information."

Eric followed the detectives to the front door and closed it behind them.

As they drove away from Eric's apartment, Clarke said, "I think I believe him, boss. The fact that he likes the public attention on Facebook anyway. Not sure about just a glass of wine with the sister."

Hamilton pursed his lips. "Hmm, yes. He does come across as quite the ladies' man. There's still something about him though, Lewis. I can't put my finger on why I don't trust him. Let's get back to the station, pronto."

The incident room was quiet when the detectives returned, a sign of deep concentration. Hamilton barged through to his office, calling for Fraser.

"Is there something wrong, sir?" she asked gingerly, once she had caught up with him.

"I'm sorry. I didn't mean to sound so abrupt out there, Kerry. Please understand when we're in the middle of a frustrating case like this one, I sometimes get a bit tense. Especially when I feel like I'm on a bloody goose chase. But please don't always take it so personally. It won't do you any favours in this office."

The athletic blonde sergeant pulled her shoulders back in response, and he smiled.

"Yes, sir. Understood, loud and clear."

"Good, take a seat. Now we've just been to see Eric Dexter, and he swears blind that his Facebook account is filled with adoring fans, most of which he doesn't know at all," Hamilton explained, as Fraser pulled a small notebook from her pocket.

"I made a few notes that I thought were important, sir. Eric Dexter is friends with Kate Wakeman and Emily Donovan on Facebook. However, I can see what you mean about them being fans. He has over two thousand friends, mainly women. And he's not very active on the account at all."

"What do you mean?" Hamilton frowned, wondering if he was the only person left in society who was not a fan of social media and the stress it constructed in people's lives.

"Every account has a Facebook wall, sir. Active members post their own statuses, photographs, and likes onto that wall. When I took a look at Eric's, there are mainly posts from other people. So fans have congratulated him on a performance or an interview. Friends have tagged him in their photographs from parties or at the theatre. But in regards to him actually posting things himself, he hasn't done so for at least six months. He also doesn't have any security set up, so you can look at anything on his profile."

"That's interesting, Kerry. I'm no expert, as you know, but I would think someone who admits they love the attention would be more interactive with their fans. Or even their friends."

"I'm not sure. Maybe he uses this account solely to pump his ego."

"You mean he could have another account?"

"Of course! It's easy to do. All you really need is a different e-mail address. There are plenty of other Kerry Frasers on Facebook," she said with a smile.

"Could you do some more digging? See if Eric Dexter has another account?"

"Definitely, sir. I can search his friends list again and see if any of them have any other Erics or Dexters on their list. I'll find out if he has a middle name. He may have used that to create a different account. And with your permission, I'll try and get into our victims' accounts, see if they had any personal communication with him."

"Brilliant!" Hamilton punched his left palm. "Of course you have my permission, Kerry. Get right on it. Give Sharon a holler if you need any help. And report back to me the minute you find something."

CHAPTER TWENTY-ONE

A white feather fell slowly in the breeze and landed at Grace's feet as she entered the cemetery. She collected it from the ground, smiled, and placed it in her pocket before making her way to her grandfather's grave.

"Hi, Granddad," she said, kneeling on the grass to tidy the flowers. "Sorry I didn't bring any fresh ones today. I came straight from work. I know you're not bothered about flowers anyway, probably hate me spending money on them. They look pretty, though."

She smiled when she thought of her grandfather's stern but loveable character. Finally, content with their appearance, Grace stopped playing with the arrangement, pulled her scarf and coat collar closer to her face, and tucked her hands in her pockets.

"I had a bad day. Well, it was okay. I was proud of myself for booking an appointment with the psychiatrist. Which I know you'll be rolling your eyes at. Why do I need to tell a complete stranger my business? What could I possibly gain from it? But like Mum says, I have to be honest with myself. I miss you terribly, and it is affecting my everyday life. My moods are... I don't even know how to explain them. I completely snapped at Michael today. You remember my boss? I can't believe I had the nerve to speak to him like that; I could lose my job. But it just came out, and I'm not entirely sure why. To be fair, he gave as good as he got. I think. The whole conversation seems like it happened days ago now, not just a few hours."

She glanced around the cemetery. Nearby a young couple were placing a bunch of bright lilies, her favourite flowers, on a grave. Tears streamed down her face. Grief overtook her, as it always did when she visited the cemetery, the last resting place for so many people, so much so she had become oblivious to her own weeping.

"I'm so scared, Granddad. Four women have been murdered. And I knew three of them! Can you believe that? What does that mean? Is it safe for me to be out right now? Is it safe for any woman to be out on her own? Well, no, obviously not with what's going on. Do you think there's a connection? Am I being watched? No, I'm being paranoid. Natasha told me there was a local stabbing; a young lad died. What a waste of a life. This city is not safe any more. It wasn't like this when you came over from Ireland to live here. I bet there were so many more stories you didn't get a chance to tell me."

Grace sat silently as the sun set below the horizon, leaving an orange glow in its wake. She looked forward to the brightness of spring because something as simple as the weather could enhance her mood. The last reflection of colour drained from the sky, and the sudden chill made her shiver. She hadn't noticed the young couple leave and quickly worried about the length of time she had sat there alone. *God, I don't want to get locked in the cemetery at night.* She pulled the white feather from her pocket and rubbed it between her thumb and fingers, hoping it would bring her safety. "I think I better go, Granddad. I'm sure you wouldn't be pleased if I stayed out in the dark much longer. I just had to talk to you."

Once she was home, Grace decided to spend time with her mother. They enjoyed a few hours watching comedy DVDs and sharing their favourite treats of chocolate, biscuits, and popcorn.

"You gave him the easy ones. Hip-hop, hip-hop…" The pair erupted in fits of giggles before Valerie could finish one of their favourite lines from the movie.

"But I wipe my own ass," Grace added, her eyes closed in amusement.

"I don't care how old I am, *Big Daddy* gets me every time." Valerie wiped joyful tears from her cheeks.

They continued to laugh together. Grace was forced to hold her stomach. Her muscles clenched from her hysterical laughing, and the pain was unbearable yet enjoyable. She realised it was the first time in weeks that she did not have the urge to reach for a bottle of wine.

"I had completely forgotten we could have this much fun." Grace bent down to kiss her mother's cheek.

"Really? Oh, I didn't, darling. I knew you'd be ready to laugh again soon enough. I just had to be patient with you. As always, you stubborn minx."

Valerie's smile was infectious, and Grace was delighted that, for a change, she was part of the reason her mother looked happy.

"Thanks, Mum. I think it's exactly what we both needed tonight."

The pair shared a hug before Grace climbed the stairs to her bedroom, where she enjoyed a calm and peaceful night's sleep.

****

Grace knocked on Michael's office door and patiently waited for an answer before she entered.

"Morning, Grace," Michael greeted her coldly.

"Morning, Michael. May I sit down?"

He gestured with his hand to the chair opposite him.

"I wanted to apologise for yesterday."

Michael finally made eye contact with her and smiled.

"It was extremely rude of me to talk to you like that. My language was not suitable, nor was my attitude. You're my manager, and it won't happen again."

"Oh, Grace!" Michael raised his hands in the air, stood up, and made his way around the desk. He perched on the edge of it so their legs were just inches apart.

"Yes, it's been an emotional time for me lately. And yes, we have some stressful situations arising here at the theatre, but that does not condone my outburst or give me the right to speak to you the way I did," Grace continued.

"You have no idea how glad I am you've apologised. Let's forget it happened." Michael clicked his fingers and placed his hand on Grace's shoulder. "It's already in the past."

Grace was glad that the apology had panned out so smoothly. She would have hated the thought of Michael holding a grudge against her and making life difficult at work. The London was a great escape from reality, or at least it had been before the New Year. The day continued with an upbeat momentum. She and Michael were working in their usual unison in preparation for opening night.

Later that afternoon, Grace turned off her computer and gathered her bag and coat. She decided to finish work early to ensure she was on time for her first session with Maria.

As she walked to the underground station, her nerves kicked in, and she fiddled with her angel pendant for comfort. The Transport for London online route planner revealed it would take her forty minutes from Covent Garden to Wembley Central Station, followed by a ten-minute walk to the psychiatrist's office. Once settled in a carriage, she took out her book, Tammy Robinson's *Charlie & Pearl*, and delved into someone else's world.

Mingled with the crowd, all restless to exit the train station, Grace fished her iPhone from her bag and opened the Maps app. She copied the postcode from her screwed-up piece of paper into her phone and chose the person symbol to get directions by foot. She turned left and watched her fellow commuters rush by, eager to get to the pub or home to their families after their working week.

After ten minutes, she found herself in a quiet, well-lit cul-de-sac. She stopped outside number twelve then slowly walked up the path to the front door; the nerves tingled inside her. Shaking, Grace put her phone back into her handbag and looked at the two doorbells. The top one was labelled with just the letter *A*, while the bottom label had gold-embossed lettering: *Maria Lee, Psychiatrist & Clinical Hypnotherapist*.

Her finger trembled as she outstretched it above her head and pressed the second bell.

A curvaceous white woman in her late fifties, with tight, curly, short blonde hair, opened the front door. Grace stepped back slightly. The woman's buoyancy surprised her, but she couldn't help but warm to the huge smile greeting her. It was contagious, and Grace was compelled to return the grin. The woman's eccentric taste was plain to see, and although the woman wore a modest dress that didn't show off too much cleavage, the mixture of purple, orange, and green colours screamed for attention. Large, vibrant beads adorned her neck and chest, adding to the jovial character.

"You must be Grace! I'm Maria, obviously." She laughed, and they shook hands. "Please, come in."

While Grace followed her up the stairs, Maria jabbered on about how she had converted the house into two apartments, keeping her home downstairs, where she had access to the garden, and transforming the upstairs into an office. Grace barely heard a word the woman said; her mind was cloudy with the decision she had made to enter a complete stranger's house. Maria led her to a large lounge at the front of the apartment, where the walls were covered in pretty paintings of puppies, kittens, oceans, sunsets, and a cornfield in the countryside. Her attention was drawn a deep-purple, rich velvet reclining chair. The type she had only seen in fashion magazines. Maria gestured to it.

"You expect me to lie down?"

Maria smiled. "Not if you don't want to. Some patients feel more comfortable looking away from me when they talk. They prefer to admire the calming artwork on the wall."

"No, thank you." Grace fiddled with the button on her coat so furiously, it came loose from the thread. She sat down and dropped her hands into her lap. "I'm sorry. I just feel very nervous. I don't know what I should be saying."

"There's no need to apologise. Please don't put extra pressure on yourself."

Maria's charming smile and kind-hearted tones were inviting, and Grace relaxed her shoulders and took off her coat.

"Grace, I'm here to help you with all those emotions and hopefully guide you into feeling comfortable in this room. Now, let me hang your coat up. Relax, and I'll make us a lovely cup of tea." As the psychiatrist bounced from the chair, her large beads clashed together from the swift movement. Maria hummed a tune Grace was unfamiliar with, cheerfully bopping her head while she walked to a small alcove in the corner of the room.

She reminds me of my crazy, fun nana. She was such a kind woman. I'll keep that image in my head. I can do this. I can open up to her.

Maria returned and handed her a mug decorated with a tabby cat playing with a ball of yarn. Grace felt warmth inside her and not just from the tea, but also from the kind stranger.

"On the phone, you told me your grandfather had passed away. I am so sorry for your loss. How did he die?" Maria asked.

"Cancer."

"That is sad. It's an awful disease that affects so many of us in different ways. What kind of a relationship did you have with him?"

"We were very close. He was a very influential person in my life." Grace paused and closed her eyes. "I'm sorry. I can't talk about my granddad. Not yet, anyway."

"That's absolutely fine. We'll take this at your pace," Maria said, retrieving a leopard-print notebook from the table.

"What's that for? Will you make notes about me?" Grace asked warily.

"Just notes about our session, dear. No need to worry. It's mainly so I remember subjects you don't want to talk about, like you've just mentioned, as well as the aspects of your life you are willing to share with me. You also said you were having trouble sleeping. Do you want to discuss that?"

"It's the nightmares," she said, expecting Maria to ask more questions. The woman nodded but remained silent, so Grace continued and explained the full nature of her dreams.

"And how do these nightmares make you feel?"

"Maria, they scare me. I wake up feeling petrified after I've had one." She stared hard into the mug, her fingers wrapped tightly around it. "I've dreamt of a dead body. A woman lying naked, covered in dirt and wet leaves. Screams echo in my ears; people beg for their lives."

"And when did they begin?"

"I'm not sure. A few months ago." She hesitated to continue.

"What is it, Grace? What are you thinking?"

"I think it all began after those young women were murdered. You see, Maria, I knew three of them," Grace whispered the last sentence. "My God, could I be next?"

The psychiatrist's eyes widened. "I'm not working on this case, so I couldn't possibly profile the killer or speak about the connection between the women. But if you feel your life could be in jeopardy because you were friends with some of the victims, then you must contact the police."

"They're aware. It just makes me wonder, how do we escape from these nutters in society? How can I truly be sure that I'm safe? How do you know that you are? That any of us are?" Grace's heartbeat increased.

"Calm down, sweetie. You're safe here," Maria said softly. "I have to believe that all of this could explain the nightmares you're experiencing. Because you knew these women, you have a sense of connection to them. Their untimely and brutal deaths have more meaning to you than they would to, say for example, me. The feelings that are attached to your subconscious could be so vivid because you can see these victims as more than just women—you see them as friends with their own personalities, hopes and dreams."

It made sense to Grace and changed her attitude. She was thankful for her mother's suggestion to see Maria. The psychiatrist wrote more notes, and Grace was glad for the short break, which gave her time to compose herself.

"Did your dreams occur before or after information was released in the press about the victims and their murders?" Maria asked.

"I'm not sure. What do you mean?"

"Newspapers, interviews and press conferences give the public a lot of detail about the victims, the crimes and the specifics that surround those murders. It's possible that your brain has picked out various points from all the information, but because it's a traumatic experience for you, the brain locks it away, so to speak. There's where your subconscious comes into play and brings it all into your sleeping state, when you're at your most vulnerable. But that's the problem with dreams—they're subliminal, so images are misinterpreted, and messages are misunderstood."

"I didn't even think of that, Maria. I can't remember when I had the first nightmare, but I found out about all the deaths from the newspaper or people telling me."

"Grace, what I would like you to do is to start keeping a diary. Use it to keep track of your nightmares, if you do have any more. List the date, what you can remember seeing, and how it made you feel."

"So will I see you again?"

"Yes, I would like that."

"I think you could definitely benefit from further sessions. We can explore the nightmares you're having and maybe talk about your grandfather when you're ready. I'm going to book an appointment for the same time next week. Will that work for you?"

Grace nodded. "Yes, it will. Obviously, I was extremely nervous about coming, but I'm glad I did. Just that little insight into my dreams and subconscious has made me feel relieved slightly." She stood up, and Maria fetched her coat.

"I'm delighted. Same time next week then."

As Maria led Grace to the front door, the woman gently touched her shoulder. "Write that diary over the next week. Even if there are no nightmares, use it to explore how you're feeling about everything in your life. And please, Grace, if you find yourself in a situation where you don't feel safe, please contact the police immediately."

"Of course. Thank you so much, Maria. I'm looking forward to next week already."

Grace's mood was lighter, and she felt confident Maria could help her through her immense amount of grief. The street was considerably quieter and darker than it had been before, and Grace determined a brisk stride was necessary for her return trip to the train station.

CHAPTER TWENTY-TWO

The team grouped together in the incident room, some perched on desks while others sat in their office chairs. DI Hamilton stood next to the whiteboard.

"I know you understand my frustration with this case because I appreciate you all feel it too. We've had four women brutally murdered in just two months and there's hardly any clues or suspects," Hamilton said with disappointment in his voice. He rubbed his hand over his eyes and face. "Let's share our updates."

Fraser, who always seemed eager to please him, spoke first. "Unfortunately, I can't find another Facebook account for Eric Dexter, sir. I was thinking, though, could he be using a completely different name?"

Clarke replied, "I don't think so, Kerry. This guy gets off on the attention of women. If he used an anonymous name, they wouldn't know it was him, Mr. Celebrity."

"No, but that could be how he chooses his victims," she argued back, and Clarke mock saluted.

"That's an interesting theory, Kerry," Hamilton interrupted. "The women were all murdered in the vicinity of his home or work. And I can't shake the feeling that Vicky Lawlor's red dress was a clue."

"Gov, while we're speaking about our Lady in Red," Morris interjected, "she worked at Cocktails and Dreams, a bar in Covent Garden. I've had a look on Google Maps, and it's about a ten-minute walk from The London Theatre."

"Of course it is." Hamilton sighed.

"Kerry's had a look, and there's no online connection between Vicky Lawlor and Eric Dexter," Morris continued. "I called the manager this morning, and he confirmed Vicky was working that night. She offered to work later than her usual shift because of the crowd for the New Year's Eve party."

Hamilton clicked his fingers. "Great progress, Sharon. I want you and Les to get down to the bar immediately and find out everything about that night. Who was working the shift with Vicky? Was anyone acting suspicious? Was she friendly with any customers?"

"Boss, how about we bring a photograph of Eric Dexter?" Wedlock said.

"Yes! Flash that around the bar. Good thinking, Les. If the theatre is just ten minutes away, they must have had after-work drinks in there at some point, right? Find out if anyone recognises him and, more importantly, remembers him talking to Vicky."

Clarke flipped through his notebook. "When we questioned Dexter, we asked if he knew Vicky Lawlor. He paused for a nanosecond but replied in the negative."

"That doesn't mean it was an honest answer." Hamilton raised his eyebrows.

Morris and Wedlock collected their coats and headed for the door, stopping briefly next to their superior.

"You think this Dexter is our guy, gov?"

Hamilton exhaled noisily. "The evidence is slim, Les, so I can't give a resounding yes, as much as I'd like to. But there's something there; I just don't trust him. He's caught up in this somehow—of that I'm sure."

Clarke stood up from the table then added the team's update and their new theory to the whiteboard.

"Lewis and Kerry, while the others are gone, I want you both to continue delving into our victims' lives. My gut is adamant that Dexter is the killer or that there's a link to the theatre at least, but I don't want to shoot myself in the foot with this one. It's imperative we're one hundred per cent sure there's no other connection between them. Dig as far as you can. I'll be in my office if you need me."

Hamilton walked away feeling confident. He relished the times when the team could ignite that spark inside him again and make him see an investigation from a different perspective or add a new concept to the mix.

He closed his office door and sat at his desk, surveying the mess that was his inbox. He decided progress in this murder case was of the utmost importance and pushed the pile of papers aside. He lifted the phone receiver and dialled a number imprinted in his memory.

"Hello, Laura Joseph—"

"Laura, it's DI Hamilton," he spoke before she had a chance to finish.

"Oh, Inspector, I'm glad you've called. It's been on my to-do list to contact you, but I'm in demand here at the moment; six fatalities from a road accident on the North Circular."

"That's awful, Laura. In that case, I won't keep you any longer than necessary. Please tell me you have an update from the clothes on our last two victims."

"I do, but I'm afraid you're not going to like it. Your killer is clever. There is no secondary DNA on either of the women's clothing."

Hamilton's jaw tightened.

"I'm sorry, Inspector, I know it's not what you wanted to hear. I must dash, goodbye."

"Thanks, Laura. Bye."

Hamilton returned the phone to its dock and slumped onto his desk. He knew he had to keep his mind busy, or he would explode inside with anger. *How does he keep evading us? What the hell am I not seeing?* He decided to rejoin Clarke and Fraser in the incident room; he was prepared to search through the case files in the hope of uncovering any missed vital evidence. He needed something that would give his team the real breakthrough they so desperately required.

CHAPTER TWENTY-THREE

Grace felt alone. She reached for her phone, opened WhatsApp, and scrolled to Natasha's contact.

Grace: Hey hun, haven't heard from u all week. How are u? X

She drummed her fingers on the phone screen and impatiently waited for the two blue ticks to appear, signalling that her message had been delivered then read by Natasha. They remained grey and ignored.

Grace: Fancy a drink? Come on, it's Saturday night and I could really do with a catch-up over a glass of wine. Or two, ha ha! Have some news about what I got up to last night... nothing saucy, obviously, LOL. X

With no blue ticks alighting, Grace's frustration grew. She threw the phone on her bed and made her way downstairs to the kitchen. She could feel her mother's eyes burning into her back as she opened the fridge to grab a bottle of wine.

"So... how did your first session with the shrink go last night, love? I didn't hear you come in and didn't want to disturb you when I got home from work earlier."

"Mum, she's a clinical psychiatrist."

"Yes, well, that's a bit of a mouthful. Anyway, tell me all about it. Do you feel better now that you've spoken to her?"

"From one session? Gosh, Mum." Grace poured herself a large glass of white wine.

"I don't know how these things work. Why don't you sit down and have your drink with me? Tell your old mum all about it. I'd really love to hear how it went."

"I'm probably meeting Natasha. We can chat about it some other time."

Grace returned the wine bottle to the fridge and left her mum in the kitchen. Her phone lit up the moment she entered the room, making her smile, and she quickly retrieved it to read the message.

Natasha: Sorry babe, I'm out with Ben. Another time for sure x

Her eyes narrowed at the screen. *Who the fuck is Ben?* Irritated further by her friend's lack of interest, she downed the entire glass of wine and returned to the kitchen to replenish it.

"Jesus, love! You made light work of that drink. Do you really think you should have another one?" Valerie questioned.

"Don't start, Mum. It's been a long week. I'm just trying to unwind."

Content once the glass was brimming to the top, Grace disregarded her mother and tapped the phone screen anxiously.

Grace: And who the hell is Ben? Can you rearrange your plans? I could really do with a chat tonight. U know, let my hair down as u keep telling me to, ha ha! x

Natasha: The guy we met at The Oak that weekend. He's scrummy. Sorry no can do, I'm already out with him. Catch up tomoz chick. X

Grace threw her phone onto the kitchen table and gulped her wine as if she hadn't enjoyed the taste for weeks rather than minutes.

"Well, I don't think that's going to solve your problems, love." Valerie glared at her daughter.

"Really, Mum? Maybe it will. It clears my head." She slammed the empty wine glass on the table.

"Alcohol does no such thing. If you think it does, it's only a temporary fix because your head is so intoxicated."

"Well, it's working for me right now." Grace reached for the bottle, intent on draining what was left of it, but Valerie whisked the glass from the kitchen table.

"Back off, Mum! I'm a grown woman! If I want to sit here and have three glasses of wine—or the whole flaming bottle, for that matter—I'm entitled to do so."

"Not under my roof, you're not. I have no intention of spending my Saturday night watching you get pissed and then cleaning vomit from your bedroom floor. Again! Grow up, for heaven's sake, Grace."

"Absolutely fine by me," she roared at her mother. "I have other friends I can have a good time with. I don't need you or Natasha. I'm going out."

"What? You already said you were going out with Natasha tonight. Has the alcohol affected you so quickly that you can't remember?"

"Well, plans change. She's all loved up and shit. No time for her friend who needs her." Grace necked the remaining dregs of white wine straight from the bottle.

"Don't wait up for me, Mum." She laughed menacingly as she left the kitchen. With no destination in mind, but knowing she had to get out of the house, Grace grasped her jacket from the coat stand and walked out the front door without closing it behind her.

CHAPTER TWENTY-FOUR

Looking out onto the river at night was so peaceful. The darkness had taken over, but the twinkling lights were still visible in the distance, and the movement of the water was comforting. This city was so busy and hectic; no one stopped to soak up the culture or enjoy the view: The London Eye, Big Ben, or the nurse walking towards the bridge. The purple uniform peeked out from under her unzipped coat, and her hair was pulled back into a neat bun.

Too busy staring at her phone, she didn't even notice me. *That's all they're bothered about—their own lives—when they should be caring for others.* She stole two minutes away from her screen and scanned the bridge. I was in the shadows, but she saw me, a lone figure looking down on her. If she were clever, she would have chosen to bypass the dark and quiet bridge and taken the long route round. I tingled inside. She chose to be brave—she chose to venture straight for me.

Hesitantly, she took the first step up. *Too late to back out.* I turned round so I was leaning on the bridge's barrier, my back facing the direction she was coming from. I fixed the hood on my jacket to hide my face. The sound of her footsteps on the stairs quickened. *She wants to run right past me. I'll let her pass. Just.*

I could smell her perfume, sweet and sickly. A few more moments, and she would be behind me. As still as a statue, I knew how to remain calm. *Damn, it's so peaceful here.* I could hear her panting as she passed, and an excited shiver slid down my back. When she was within reach of the stairs that would take her to the other side of the riverbank, I knew she must have felt safe—almost free.

Two giant leaps were all it took to stand right behind her. She tried to scream, but I covered her mouth and took the sound before she had a chance to make it. My leather glove smothered her face, and I pulled her hair so tightly, she had no choice but to lean backwards. I dragged her back to the middle of the bridge. *She's stronger than the others.*

I let her go briefly, and she turned to face me. *Why didn't you run, stupid bitch?* Before the thought of fleeing could enter her mind, my fist connected with her stomach, and she doubled over, eyes wide in pain. Her nose cracked as it met the force of my knee and sent her crashing onto the ground. She cried like a baby—and disturbed my fucking peace—so I booted her in the face. Twice. That shut her up.

Blood seeped from her nose and mouth. Her eyes spun to the back of her head, but she couldn't fight it for long; death was knocking. She closed her eyes. I delivered forceful blows to her chest and stomach with my boot. She was limp, and I kicked her over onto her back then undid the buttons of her clothes.

"You're meant to care for people—that's your profession. But you don't. You're selfish and cruel, and you must be punished."

I knelt, peering at her naked chest, barely moving as her breathing became slower, almost non-existent. I reached into my pocket for the knife. I didn't slow down. I didn't think. I thrust the blade deep into her chest—into her heart.

The rush was a release for me, and I wanted to shout it out, let it flow from me, and roar loudly that I was there. But I needed to remain in control; that was my ultimate goal. I gripped the knife impaled in her chest and didn't move. The power was immense. *All this strength is in my hands, and I refuse to let go of this feeling.*

CHAPTER TWENTY-FIVE

Hamilton stopped briefly on the top step of the bridge, while Clarke walked on. He scanned the area, looking out onto the beauty of London's iconic sights and landmarks. He was stunned, and devastated, that another woman's body had been discovered in such a usually crowded area.

"He's stepped up his level of violence again, Detectives," Laura explained when Hamilton rejoined his partner. "I hope you don't have weak stomachs."

"Where's the witness who found the body?" Hamilton asked immediately.

"He's downstairs with uniform. Quite shaken up, as you can imagine. He stayed with the body until we arrived. Can't have been easy, given the state she's in."

"Lewis, get down there and take his statement now while it's still fresh. Get all the information you can. Did he see anyone else lurking around? Is he usually out jogging so early on a Sunday morning?"

Clarke's eyes widened and he headed for the stairs. "Gov, it's not my first interview," he said over his shoulder.

"Apologies for my partner. He's not really a morning person."

Laura snorted a response, and Hamilton knew best to leave it at that.

"Step into my office, Denis."

The pair walked into the white tent that covered the width of the bridge. A member from Laura's team was busy taking photographs of the body.

"Tight squeeze, eh?" Hamilton jested in a bid to break the tension.

"It's imperative we get as much information from the scene, so suck it up for a few minutes."

He regretted the sarcasm when he caught sight of the victim's bruised and battered naked body.

"The blood on the ground indicates blunt-force head trauma, but obviously, that doesn't necessarily mean it was the cause of death. My attention is drawn to the injuries on her face and torso; he was brutal this time. Kicked and punched her numerous times. I won't know until the post-mortem if these occurred before or after death, but I'd guess the former." Laura's eyes lingered on the woman's multiple chest wounds. "Looks like you've got yourself a serial killer, Inspector."

"Thanks for the summary, Laura. I doubt I'll be able to send anyone over to the post-mortem. Can you contact me as soon as it's done? Maybe there'll be the mark of a footprint we can use or finally some DNA. As he was obviously infuriated, he might have slipped up this time. Is that okay?"

"Of course. I'm getting my team to wrap up here now. We've had a perimeter search of the bridge but haven't found anything, not even the victim's personal effects. Perhaps he's intending to make you work harder on this one." Laura winced, and Hamilton felt the valid blow of her observations.

"Just what I need. Thanks, Laura. I'll be in touch."

Hamilton descended the stairs of the bridge in search of Clarke. He soon found his partner with a tall white man wearing tight black Lycra shorts.

"Boss, this is Charlie Fenton. He found the body."

"I'm Detective Inspector Denis Hamilton. What can you tell us, Mr. Fenton?"

"That's my old man's title. Please call me Charlie."

Hamilton was disturbed by the man's grin. He raised his eyebrows for the man to answer his question; he wasn't interested in playing name games.

"Erm… I'm local to the area, and this is my jogging route. Come rain or shine, I'm out pounding the streets because I'm training for the marathon. Just a few months left," Charlie explained.

"What time did you get to the bridge?"

"About five a.m. like I do every morning. I usually double back over this bridge and make my way home. Except this morning, I got the fright of my life."

"And you called 999 immediately?"

"Of course I did, Inspector."

"How?"

"Excuse me?"

"How did you make the call? Excuse me for pointing this out, but there doesn't seem much room for a mobile phone in those shorts." Hamilton smirked but intently observed the man's reaction to his question.

"I used that payphone over there. Is there a problem?"

He followed to where Charlie pointed. A row of traditional red public phone booths stood on the other side of the pavement. He made a note to check if they were monitored by CCTV.

"Did you see anyone suspicious, anyone lurking around the bridge?" Hamilton asked.

"No. Hardly ever do, really. Even for the heart of the city, a four a.m. start is early. And what with it being the weekend, I'm sure most residents are still in bed with a hangover." The man chuckled.

"You sound confident you were definitely alone."

Charlie frowned. "Inspector, I don't understand. Have I done something wrong? As I've said, I run the area every morning. It's usually quiet, and I see very few people. I called the police as soon as I saw that poor woman lying in a pool of blood. Should I have continued running past her?"

"No, of course not. You made the right decision," Hamilton replied. "We'll need you to come down to the station to make an official statement. Is that okay?"

"Of course, Inspector. As long as I can get a lift home afterwards. As you said, these shorts hardly have pockets for cash."

"DS Clarke will arrange uniform police to escort you. Thank you for your time." He shook the man's hand and turned to his partner. "I'll wait for you by the cars."

Hamilton heard the two men exchange pleasantries as he turned to walk away. Rage soared through his veins. *Another poor woman murdered.*

"That was a bit harsh," Clarke said when he approached.

"What are you talking about?"

"I'm surprised you didn't inspect his palms for bloodstains, boss. For one second, I thought you were going to arrest him there and then."

"Don't be dramatic, Lewis."

"Come on, what happened back there?"

Hamilton sighed. "I'm not sure. I'm just wracked with guilt for these women, and if I'm honest, that Charlie Fenton seemed a bit creepy."

"I thought he was kind of cool. He's running the marathon for Cancer Research UK."

"Hmm, yes, well, that doesn't discount the fact that he's the first civilian to discover one of our murder victims. He also used a payphone to inform us, the same way we've found out about the other women, except this time, he stayed. Coincidence, possibly."

"What are you saying, boss? Now you think he's our murderer?"

"No, that's not what I said. But right now, everything is a clue. This killer is upping the ante with every victim. What's not to say now he's sticking round to watch us in action."

Clarke chuckled, but Hamilton was in no laughing mood.

"Well, like I said, I thought he seemed like a nice guy."

"Then let's hope you're right, Lewis."

A silence fell between the partners, but Hamilton couldn't afford to entice Clarke's sulking nature.

"Look, let's head back to the station and collate all this information. We won't have information about the victim's identity or DNA until Laura's finished at the mortuary, and who knows how long that will be. So let's not call the team in just yet. Does that work for you, Lewis?"

"Your call, boss. As you've pointed out already, there's not much they can do right now, so let's not ruin their Sunday, as well."

It was too late; Clarke's teenage tantrum was brewing, but Hamilton chose to ignore it. The men drove in separate cars, much to Hamilton's delight. The thought of sharing a journey with his partner's foul mood was exhausting. However, he was pleased to find Clarke joking with Fred, the desk sergeant, when he arrived.

"Ah, Detective Inspector Hamilton. How nice of you to grace us with your presence on a Sunday," Fred said, laughing at his own joke.

"Not out of choice, believe me." Hamilton mocked a large yawn.

"I bet not. Is it anything to do with this note left for you?"

"What note?" Hamilton and Clarke chimed in harmony.

Fred handed over a handwritten note.

"How bloody long has this been sitting here?" Hamilton bellowed.

"I've only just come on duty at six a.m., sir. Which means it would have been taken by William, the desk sergeant working last night's shift."

Hamilton scanned the note. "Jesus, Fred! This says eleven p.m. on it. I think someone should have made more of an effort to get this in the hands of a superior officer!"

"With all due respect, if we desk sergeants spent all our time chasing information from people who walked in off the street, we'd get no work done. And in William's defence, I don't think there's much more he could have done. You're lucky he knows about your case and left a note directly for you." The desk sergeant stood firm in his convictions, but Hamilton noticed a slight flustered tinge appear in his cheeks.

"You're right, Fred. I know you deal with some crap down here. The reason we're here so early on a weekend is because we've just been called to another murder in Central London. The victim had no identification on her, so I just hope it wasn't this girl," Hamilton said, backhanding the piece of paper.

"What the hell does it say, gov?" Clarke called out.

"Lewis, we need coffee! Let's go over this upstairs." Hamilton walked towards the security door and waited to be buzzed in. "Thanks again, Fred."

Hamilton took the stairs two at a time with Clarke on his tail. When they reached the incident room, he handed the note to his partner as he flipped the switch on the kettle.

"Shit! Gov, do you think it's the same woman?"

"I don't know, Lewis. I think we need to call the team in now. I'll clear the overtime, and you can tell them that when you phone them. I don't see it being a problem, not when it comes to this case."

"I get the short straw of calling the guys in on a Sunday morning, do I? Nice delegating," Clarke said light-heartedly.

"Hey, feel free to put the overtime request in with DCI Allen instead," Hamilton retorted, then laughed at his partner's silence. "No, I didn't think so."

Over the course of the next hour, the rest of the team trickled into the incident room. In that time Clarke, fueled with coffee, had updated the information board. Hamilton entered the office with a tray of bacon rolls, much to the pleasure of his sleepy-looking team.

"Thanks for coming in on such short notice, and on a Sunday. I really appreciate your hard work. I've squared the overtime with the powers that be, so don't worry about that. Now, tuck into these while I update you on this morning's turn of events."

Hamilton brought their attention to the updated information and tapped the board as he explained what had been uncovered on the bridge over the River Thames. "When we arrived back at the station, I had the following note left for me by last night's desk sergeant." He pulled out the note and read aloud. "Detective Inspector Hamilton, I wanted to make you aware of a young lady that came into the station tonight, at approximately eleven p.m. She was highly intoxicated, swaying and slurring her words. She kept repeating "Eric attacked me. Eric attacked me, but I escaped." When I asked for more information, she wouldn't give me any, except that her name was Carly. I offered to call one of the senior officers down, and that's when she ran from the station. I didn't get a good look at her face, as she was wearing a cap and sunglasses—yes, at night, but as already stated, she was extremely drunk. Had heard snippets about your latest case, so thought you might like to know about it."

Hamilton paused to look at his team. He was met with puzzled expressions and wide eyes. "So what do you think of that?"

Morris spoke first. "You're thinking Eric Dexter, sir?"

"That's exactly what I'm thinking, Sharon. I also can't help but worry that this could be the same girl who was found brutally murdered a few hours ago."

"I can't believe he didn't try and get more information from the girl. Or at least note down what she was wearing, her height, something!" Fraser added. "How about I look over the station's CCTV, gov? I should easily be able to identify this woman from the footage; drunk girl in sunglasses at eleven p.m. won't be too hard to trace. At least that way, we can ascertain her build and what she was wearing. Might help ID the victim too."

"Kerry, that's brilliant. Glad to see someone's on top form this morning." Hamilton clicked his fingers. "Sharon and Les, I want you both to get over to the mortuary now. Laura won't be expecting you now, but that shouldn't be a problem. Hang round like irritating bugs if you have to, but don't leave without the information from our latest victim. Lewis, I think we need to pay another visit to Mr. Dexter and find out if he knows who this Carly is."

"Boss, why don't we bring him in to the station for questioning this time? The surprise tactic might force him into telling us what he's really been up to with these women," Clarke suggested.

Hamilton mulled the idea over. "Lewis, I like your way of thinking. Get on to uniform and tell them to pick him up. I'll be in my office, gathering all the information we have so far for his interview. If he's got something to hide, then this type of approach will highlight that."

CHAPTER TWENTY-SIX

At that moment, Grace couldn't think of anything less appealing than the Sunday matinee performance, which had become expected since Michael had introduced the idea for new plays at The London. He invited local businesses and the press to watch the show, believing that word of mouth would spark excitement for the main opening night the following day.

"Where the hell have you been? The performance began twenty minutes ago," Michael whispered, his face contorted with anger.

"I'm so sorry. I don't feel very well this morning," Grace replied, as she wiped sweat from her brow.

Michael gasped. "Please do not tell me you're hungover!" He left the viewing area and pulled Grace into the corridor.

"I only went out for a few drinks last night. It was stupid. I know how important these matinees are to you. I'm really sorry; it won't happen again."

"Important to me? They're important to everyone here, to the whole team. These matinees are an advertisement for the main show. It gets people talking. I expected more from you, Grace. I'm really disappointed."

She could feel Michael's eyes fixed on her, the anger radiating from them, but she didn't have the courage to make eye contact with him. "I know. I'm sorry," she mumbled, twiddling her fingers round each other.

He tutted. "Gosh, I'm not saying don't have fun on the weekends. Even I had a few drinks last night. But in all honesty, Grace, to turn up to work looking like this, you should be ashamed. Now get yourself into makeup. Only that can help with that ghastly appearance. And drink some water. I need you looking your beautiful self by the time the performance finishes. We're dealing with the press together." Michael stormed back to his prime position backstage, where he had a view of the play unfolding and the audience's reaction.

Grace slumped her shoulders, completely embarrassed, and wandered down the corridor as she had been instructed to do.

"Gorgeous!" Michael squealed with excitement when she returned after the performance. "That's the Grace we all know and love. How are you feeling?"

"Much better, thanks. Just embarrassed, really. And disappointed that I missed the show. How did it go?"

Michael waved his hand, dismissing her comment. "Don't worry about all that, Grace. I understand the importance of letting your hair down on the weekend. I'm not an ogre. As I said, I did myself last night. I just recover better than you."

She managed to fake her best smile while Michael chuckled.

"Anyway, our civilian audience are exiting the theatre while the local press congregates in the bar. We'll take questions in there. It seems more relaxed and informal." He leaned in closer and spoke softly. "I'm sure the vultures will slip in questions about the name change and that murdered girl, and our own poor Emily, of course. But ignore them. Do you understand? I'll answer those with short and swift replies, force them to focus on the actual performance. There's bound to be some jumped-up new journalist trying his luck; I know it."

She could sense Michael's annoyance, and despite the makeup crew's fantastic job covering her external tenderness, her head was still throbbing.

"Why don't we invite some of the actors to join us? It might help take the attention off the recent news articles and redirect it to their personal characters," Grace suggested.

"No! I've never seen Blake interact with the press, and this is not the time for slip-ups." His sharp retort startled her.

"What? Blake is still in the lead role? I was sure Eric would have returned by now, especially for the matinee performance. He loves attention from the locals."

"Please, Grace, don't even get me started on that man! I've had it up to here," Michael said, raising his hand above his head. "I'm beginning to think he's more trouble than he's worth."

She chewed her bottom lip for a few seconds. "Have you spoken to him?"

"Of course I have! We decided Blake would perform the matinee show and Eric would use today to pull his bloody act together. He'll be back with us tomorrow for opening night. I just hope he doesn't mess up because of the time off he's had."

"Good. That's a relief."

Michael's nostrils flared, and his eyebrows knitted together.

Oh God, did that make it sound like I'm desperate to see Eric? "And by relief, I meant that I'm up to speed with everything. I'm sure the press will be eager to know where he is," she quickly added.

"Yes, I suppose." His face relaxed. "We'll just say he's been having some personal time and he's all set for opening night. End of."

Grace was eager to get home and crawl into bed. "I'll leave you to take care of all the answers, Michael. I'm happy to stand on the sidelines for support, though."

Michael slipped his arm around her waist and led her down the corridor towards the bar. "Don't be daft, young lady. In this theatre, you're just as important as those on the stage, and I need you right there next to me where you belong. Now, let's go tackle the hounds."

CHAPTER TWENTY-SEVEN

Energy buzzed through the incident room as keyboards were drummed and telephones rang, despite it being Sunday evening. Fraser was glued to her computer, Clarke was on the phone, and Hamilton was concentrating on the post-mortem reports, desperate to pluck something new from them.

"Boss, that was the desk sergeant," Clarke called out. "They've got Dexter downstairs waiting for us."

"Brilliant. Have you had any news from Sharon and Les?"

"They're on their way back from the mortuary. From what they said on the phone, Laura prioritised the latest victim to assist us with our investigation."

"Good, we need all the help we can get. Kerry, any luck with the CCTV footage from the front desk?"

"Not really, sir. I have found a woman who I believe to be Carly on our cameras, but there's no angle giving me a full image of her face. I've captured a screenshot, the best I could manage anyway."

Fraser got up from her desk and retrieved the photo from the printer. She gave the copy to Hamilton and Clarke, who stared at the grainy image.

"Like I said, sir, best I could do. She was only there for four minutes, so we're lucky we got the information we did from William. And he was right: she swayed about around the reception area the entire time she was there. Despite that, she never once looked directly at the camera, sorry."

"It's better than nothing. We can see what she was wearing that night and guesstimate her height. I'll show this to Dexter during the interview anyway, see what his reaction is."

Morris and Wedlock entered the incident room with huge grins on their faces, much to Hamilton's delight.

"Gov, we've got the identification of our latest victim," Morris explained, throwing her bag and coat on the table. She reached for the notebook inside her blazer pocket. "Miss Chloe Ronald, aged twenty-five, working at the Soho Centre for Health and Care."

"Bloody hell! That's brilliant, Sharon. But how did you find all that out so quickly?" Hamilton asked.

Wedlock answered, "Well, when we got to the mortuary, the team explained they had found the victim's belongings after all. Although they believed a complete sweep of the area had been conducted, as they left the bridge, one of the team spotted her bag and clothes. It looks like our killer tried lugging them over the bridge, but he missed the river and they landed a few yards further up the bank. Can you bloody believe that?"

Hamilton screwed up his face. "I'm not sure what to make of it, Les. That type of behaviour isn't the norm for our guy. He doesn't make mistakes. And why didn't he want us to have her identity, like he has with the others?"

"It also means this Carly girl is still out there," Clarke added, pointing to the photograph. "Plus, we can't even be sure that Eric Dexter is the same Eric this drunk woman was talking about. It could be a coincidence, boss."

"I take your point on board, Lewis. But I don't want to discount the fact that Dexter knew three of the victims and was in a relationship with one of them." Hamilton rubbed his hand up and down his face for a few seconds. "What else could Laura tell you from the post-mortem, Les?"

"Similar setup, gov. No rigor had set in, so time of death was no more than three hours before she was discovered. That gives us a window of roughly two a.m. to five a.m. Cause of death was the stab wounds to the heart, made with the same murder weapon used on the other victims. She also confirmed that this victim took a violent beating, and although she would have been unconscious by time the knife attack actually happened, she suffered greatly.

Still no traces of DNA and no obvious signs of sexual assault. Frustratingly, all the information we've had already."

"That's another thing that bugs me, boss. Eric Dexter is blatantly a ladies' man, so it strikes me odd that there's no sexual aspect to these crimes, if he's our guy," Clarke observed.

Hamilton pursed his lips and groaned. "Well, he's here now, so no harm in questioning; we can gauge his reaction first-hand to the news of this victim. But I want to make him stew just a little longer; let's see what that tells us about his character. Oh, and don't get comfortable, you lot. Sharon and Les, I want you to inform Chloe Ronald's family while Lewis and I interview Dexter. Kerry, delve into her life to build a picture of who she was, and that includes any connection to theatres or our only suspect downstairs."

The two detectives entered Interview Room One to find Eric huffing loudly and pacing the small room.

"Finally! I've been in here for almost an hour. You can't treat me like this. What about my rights?" Eric shouted.

"Mr. Dexter, you're here of your own free will. We thank you for coming in to help us with our enquiries and sincerely apologise for the delay you've had." Hamilton forced a smile he hoped looked genuine.

"My own free will!" Eric's voice rose. "That's not the way I was made to feel by your officers. They practically pushed me into their squad car outside my home. What the hell will my neighbours think?"

"Then it's my duty to apologise again, Mr. Dexter. I would hate to think that anyone helping us with our enquiries would be made to feel so disrespected. DS Clarke, please find out who the attending officers were so we can take this matter further." Hamilton caught the grin on his partner's face as he looked down to make a note for Eric's benefit.

"Fine, Detective. What is this all about anyway? I've waited long enough."

"Please take a seat, Mr. Dexter, and we'll get started. We just have a few more questions regarding our murder investigations."

Eric sighed, pulled out the chair, allowing the metal legs to screech against the tiled floor, and plopped into the seat. Hamilton had already instructed Clarke not to record the interview. He wanted it to remain informal, to entice the suspect to talk. He had, however, requested detailed notes from his partner. He shuffled a pile of papers, stopping to look at a few notes, and sighed. It was how he created tension; he didn't want the suspect thinking he was a pushover. As Eric's groans became louder and more exaggerated, Hamilton's mouth curved into a slight smile. *One-nil to me, sucker.*

"Mr. Dexter, where were you last night, between the hours of midnight and five a.m.?"

"At home, of course," he answered swiftly.

"Can anyone corroborate that for you?"

"No. I was home alone, going over my lines. I've missed a lot of rehearsal time, and it's opening night tomorrow."

"Do you know a Chloe Ronald?"

"No."

Hamilton noted the quick response. He flicked through another file and retrieved a photograph Fraser had printed—Chloe's Facebook profile picture. Hamilton slid it across the table towards Eric, who didn't touch it but looked at it briefly.

"Well, I don't know her." Eric scowled.

Hamilton pushed another photograph across the table, quietly observing his suspect.

"Yeah, she looks familiar. I think she works in a bar near the theatre."

"That's Vicky Lawlor. When we questioned you at your home, you said you didn't know her," Hamilton said.

"Well, I don't know her, obviously. Otherwise, I would have recognised her name when you mentioned it. She served me my drinks, but I never really spoke to her. I only knew her by her face. A pretty face too." He winked at Clarke.

"She's a murder victim, Mr. Dexter. Do you think this is funny?" Clarke barked.

The suspect quickly wiped the smile from his face, looked down, and shook his head.

Hamilton eyed his partner and winked. "Do you know anyone by the name of Carly, Mr. Dexter?"

Eric snapped his head back up. "No, I do not, and if you've found another woman who is my friend on Facebook, don't try and use that against me again. I've told you I don't know them all."

"Just one last photograph we'd like you to have a look at, Mr. Dexter. See if anything is familiar to you, please." Hamilton handed over the grainy image taken from the CCTV footage, forcing the man to take hold of it.

Eric studied the photograph for a few moments before throwing it onto the table with the others. He pushed them all back to Hamilton. "This image is awful. What exactly are you expecting me to tell you? Why are you asking me these questions?"

"I apologise for the quality of the image, but do you recognise the outfit she's wearing or anything else about her?" Hamilton replied, ignoring Eric's second question.

"No. I recognise nothing about her. To tell you the truth, I wouldn't have even been one hundred per cent sure it was a woman if you hadn't told me. Now, what the hell is this all about?"

"Would you mind giving us a DNA swab, Mr. Dexter?"

"What? No way! This has got to be some kind of joke. Are you accusing me of something? I think I want my solicitor present." Eric stood with such force that his chair crashed to the ground.

"Calm down and take a seat, sir." Clarke also rose from his chair.

"Please, Mr. Dexter, this will actually benefit you," Hamilton added.

"And how do you work that out?" Eric whined as he retrieved the chair but refused to sit down. Clarke remained standing too.

"I can completely understand your frustrations, and you're welcome to have your solicitor present whenever you wish, of course." Hamilton's calm voice defused the heated situation, and Eric returned to his seat, followed by Clarke.

He continued, "You have to understand our constant need to question you, Mr. Dexter, as you were in a relationship with one of the victims in our murder investigation." Hamilton held up his hand to stop Eric from interrupting. "By voluntarily agreeing to a DNA swab now, you're proving you have nothing to hide from us. It also allows us to exclude you from any future enquiries, meaning less of an inconvenience for you."

Eric glanced up at the ceiling, running his hands through his dark hair. Silence drifted through the room, and finally, Eric locked his eyes on Hamilton. "Of course I have nothing to hide, and of course I want to help. It just seems a lot to ask of me when I've done nothing wrong."

Hamilton returned the stare with a smug countenance. Concluding there was a selfish streak in Eric's personality, he was confident he knew exactly what decision his suspect would make.

The man held his hands up. "Okay, fine, Inspector, you win. If giving you my DNA sample means you'll leave me alone and spend your time tracking down Emily's killer, then I'll do it."

"Thank you, Mr. Dexter, we appreciate your cooperation. Right, that's it from us then. Stay right here, and someone will be along shortly to take your sample. Then you're free to go home," Hamilton explained.

Clarke leaned towards Eric as he rose from his chair. Hamilton cleared his throat to gain his partner's attention. He knew the wink from Eric had bugged Clarke, but in all honesty, he knew it was a remark Clarke was also likely to make about a pretty woman. The detectives made their way back to the front desk, and Hamilton requested a DNA sample to be taken from Eric.

"What did you think of his reaction to the request, boss?"

"Well, it was either very clever because he knows we've found no DNA on the victims and this move paints him as a law-abiding citizen, or he really does have nothing to hide. Come on, I sent the team home before we started the interview. Let's bloody well follow suit."

Clarke nodded, and the men walked outside the station to the car park.

"Do you still think Dexter_s guilty?"

Hamilton used the key fob to unlock the car and opened the driver's door. With one foot inside, he looked over the car roof. "I think he's guilty of something, and I've got to trust my instinct, partner."

CHAPTER TWENTY-EIGHT

The full moon shone brightly through a black sky. Grace sat at her bedroom window, peering out, lost in her thoughts. A sudden clatter disturbed her, and she stood up to get a better look at the pavement. A dark figure flashed by lightning quick, and she wasn't sure what it was, or if in fact it hadn't been a figment of her imagination. She held her breath, listening intently as she scanned the front garden. There was nothing. She exhaled deeply but found it difficult to tear her eyes away from the window. The wind whipped the trees, forming shadows on the road that danced aggressively under the streetlamps. The eerie darkness made her shudder, and she forced herself to walk away.

Grace thought of Maria's suggestion to make notes in a diary. She felt guilty that she had neglected to do as she had been asked thus far. She reached under her pillow and retrieved the pink notebook she had purchased specially for that purpose. She took one last look out of her window. Content there was nothing out there, she settled on top of the bed and began writing.

Sunday 31 January 2016
I haven't had any nightmares recently. Thankfully. But for some reason, I can't shake the feeling that I'm not always alone. What if someone is watching me? I'm just on edge most of the time. Even now, there was a rattle in the street, and I automatically think there's something sinister happening. Like someone is watching me or spying on my home. But that's ridiculous, and now I'm actually writing it down, I feel like an idiot. Sheesh, I'm glad I haven't voiced this to anyone. They would think I've gone crazy. Of course I'm going to get spooked, what with everything that's happening at the moment, but

surely I'm not alone in that reaction. I am not the only person who knew these women. I have to remember that. We live in a devastating world of sick people who harm and destroy its innocence. Maybe my university friends had the right idea when they upped and moved out of London. Into the countryside where it's safe and peaceful. But that's never been me, never been what I wanted from my life. I can't let the bullies of this world force me into feeling scared at every noise I hear. Yes, I'll be extra vigilant of course, but come on, Grace, pull yourself together.

She laughed, ripped the pages from the book, and threw them into the bin. She didn't want Maria thinking she was vulnerable and possibly postpone her bereavement sessions. However, she also worried the psychiatrist would chastise her for ignoring the advice to introduce the diary into her life.

Sunday 31 January 2016
I'll see Eric tomorrow. Jesus, it hasn't even been that long, but I feel so nervous. I made a stupid mistake with him, and now that so much has happened in between, how will I put things right? He'll be emotional and grieving, that is undisputable, but I must ensure that I remain professional when I'm around him. I'll sing it like a mantra to myself tomorrow: stay professional, stay professional! Do not attempt to comfort him.

Grace slipped the diary back under her pillow, satisfied that she would have at least one entry written for her next session with Maria. Once she'd dimmed the lights, pulled back the duvet and got into bed, sleep greeted her swiftly. She drifted off, exhausted.

CHAPTER TWENTY-NINE

Opening night at The London was always a hive of activity: thespians performing, costume crew helping with mid-act changes, and sound designers organising pre-show and intermission music mixes. As assistant director, Grace had planned the schedule for the performance and, therefore, had no choice but to interact with Eric.

"Here's the updated segment timings for tonight. Will you be able to handle it?" she said, handing him the film.

He avoided eye contact. "I'll have to be. It's opening night, my time to shine."

"Blake has rehearsed with these timings; he could open if it's too much for you."

Eric snapped his head up. A flash of anger glinted in his eyes.

"This is my play, goddammit! How could you even suggest that, Grace? Yes, I've missed a few weeks, but technically, we should've opened in January. I was ready then, and I'm ready now."

"I'm sorry, Eric." She shifted her gaze away from him, feeling uncomfortable. "I'm just aware, as your superior, that you're going through a lot at the moment. Plus, you look like you've hardly slept. With everything that has happened in the past few months, this opening night is extremely important for The London."

"It's bloody important to me too. The police hauled me in for questioning yesterday, and I wasn't released until late last night. I feel wrecked. I hope the makeup crew can help with these." Eric pointed to the bags under his eyes.

"Really, they questioned you? Why?"

"Oh, I don't know. To eliminate me from their enquiries, apparently."

Eric explained the previous night's events as the pair walked through the busy corridor, where crew members ran frantically from room to room, preparing for the show. They settled in the quieter auditorium.

"Well, I think that's a positive thing, Eric. It means you won't be continually harassed by them. They'll know you're not the killer because they have your DNA now."

"Yeah, that's why I gave in to their request. It just reminds me that there is a killer out there. Someone did murder Emily."

Tears shimmered in Eric's eyes, and unable to maintain her professional façade any longer, Grace placed her arm around his shoulder.

"What happened to Emily is devastating, Eric. I'm truly sorry for your loss," she said.

"Emily was a gorgeous young girl, and we had so much fun together. I know we weren't officially an item, but she meant a lot to me. We were both aware that we flirted with other people…"

Grace pulled away from Eric and took a few paces backwards. This was not the conversation she had wanted to get into.

"Oh, crap! Grace, I'm sorry. Look, about that night…"

"Stop! There's no need to talk about it. Actually, I'd prefer if we didn't."

"Okay, that's fine. I just want you to know that I had fun."

Her eyes widened. "What? How dare you dust it off so lightly, Eric? Don't you care about people's feelings? About *my* feelings?"

"Of course I do. That's way I want you to know I enjoyed myself with you. I mean hey, when I'm out of this grieving period, maybe we could go for a drink again."

"Your girlfriend was murdered while you slept in a bed with me, for Christ's sake. You insensitive moron. I can't believe I actually had feelings for you."

"You had feelings for me? Oh wow, I didn't realise, Grace. I thought it was just a bit of fun for you too."

"Seriously? Out of everything I just said, that's the one thing you heard?"

"Don't get emotional. I heard you. I'm devastated—of course I am. Isn't that obvious? But there's not much I can do about what happened that night. I know Emily was with other friends that evening, just like I was. Look, this conversation isn't going how I had planned it to."

"No, it's bloody not. Actually, I wish you had dropped this subject when I asked you to. I'm disgusted at your cold-heartedness. But angrier at myself for ever fancying you."

"Let's not argue. We can work this out, babe."

"Babe!"

Her heart hardened. The pet name that had once evoked a flutter in the pit of her stomach made her feel cheap and used. She stormed past Eric, desperate to get away from him, but he grabbed her arm and pulled her back to face him.

"Grace, don't leave like this. We can still have some good times together." He winked.

"I wouldn't want to spend time with you now if you were the last man on earth."

"Ha! You're the one who has feelings for me, lady."

She felt the heat burn her cheeks and immediately regretted declaring her affections for him. "*Had* feelings, note the past tense. I'm ashamed of myself for being sucked into your performance, it would appear you give them on *and* off the stage. I was unprofessional, and my job means everything to me. I can't believe I almost allowed you to jeopardise that. You're a selfish jerk, Eric Dexter."

Grace held her head high as she marched past him, his laughter filling the auditorium.

****

That evening, when Grace had finally made it home after more press releases, photo shoots, and celebrating a successful opening night, she was glad that her mother was already in bed. She felt drained, mainly from her altercation with Eric, and wasn't in the mood to recap over a midnight cuppa.

In her bedroom, she changed into her pink flannel pyjamas and climbed straight into bed, eager to relax and let sleep take over her body.

Tuesday 2 February 2016 – five a.m.!!!
Well, I didn't get much sleep before the nightmare returned. It was dark, pitch-black, actually. I was being followed. I didn't see anyone, but I could sense I wasn't alone. I wanted to scream when I woke up, but I couldn't, I was too scared. Scared in my own room! Once I had turned the light on, I peered round the room, scanning everywhere, but of course no one was there. It felt so real, like someone was standing right in this room watching me. I've had this feeling before, but quickly dismissed it, thought I was being paranoid. I'm calmer now, but I know there's no chance of going back to sleep. What if I close my eyes and it happens again? God, no!! Even the thought of it makes me shudder. The last thing I want to do is go into work feeling like this. It was a late night, and now I feel as if I've had no rest. No, I have to stop this pity party!! I'm sure the entire team will be knackered. I have to give 100% for them. As the saying goes… the show must go on… Ha ha! Deep down I know it's because I don't want to see Eric again. I've seen a different side to him!! What an arse-hole!! That's men for you, I guess – only interested in what they can get. I just wish it hadn't made me feel so cheap.

Grace jumped out of bed, deciding the best thing to do was shower, dress, and face the day without feeling sorry for herself. She slipped the diary into its usual place, made her bed, and mentally left her miserable feelings there with it.

"Good morning, darling. You're up bright and early," Valerie greeted her when she entered the kitchen.

"Morning, Mum. It's not out of choice, trust me, so don't be too cheery." She kissed her on the cheek and smiled.

"So how was opening night?"

"Thankfully, it went very smoothly, no hiccups. We received major praise afterwards, and Eric stole the show, despite his recent absence." Her mouth twisted at the sheer mention of his name.

"What's that face for?" Valerie chuckled.

"Oh, nothing really. Just funny how some people can bounce back so quickly from whatever life throws at them, that's all."

"Life is a rollercoaster. You just gotta ride it."

Grace sighed. "Mum, stop! I don't like it when you answer me in song at the best of times, but it's way too early for that crap today."

Valerie fake-cried before making them both a cup of tea and some toast. They spent the next thirty minutes sharing breakfast and talking about their respective evenings. Leaving the house together, Grace gave her mother a kiss and waved her off as she drove away. She then walked the ten minutes to the underground station. Tiredness set in during her train journey, and she began to wish she hadn't bolted from the comfort of her bed so quickly. She picked up a discarded Metro newspaper and was shocked to read an article about another young woman, Chloe Ronald, who'd been murdered over the weekend.

"Oh dear, did you know the girl?"

Grace looked across the carriage to find a chubby black lady offering her a tissue. She wasn't even aware of the tears wetting her cheeks and gladly accepted.

"She was a local girl. Did you know her?" the kind stranger asked again.

"No, I didn't. Thankfully."

The woman frowned, and Grace realised her answer sounded rude. Before she had a chance to explain herself, the commuter launched into a one-sided conversation.

"You're right, we should be thankful it's not someone we know. But sadly, she is someone's daughter, sister, friend, or even mother. What are the police doing about this crazed killer on the loose? That's what I'd like to know. All these women dying at the hands of a madman, and they've arrested no one. Makes me livid. How many more have to die?"

Grace nodded in agreement hoping the woman's question was a rhetorical one. She didn't know how to respond, but thankfully the woman accepted her silence and returned to reading her own newspaper. Grace stared at the pitch-black window as they raced underground, her glum reflection glaring back at her. She hadn't read about any arrests, either, but she knew the police had pulled Eric in for questioning. *Is he a suspect?*

CHAPTER THIRTY

Hamilton collected the case notes and paced the incident room. He noticed the team kept themselves busy rather than looking him directly in the eye. The call came from DCI Allen's secretary informing him that the chief was ready for him. He raced from the room, evidence in hand.

"Go straight in," Betty instructed when he arrived in the reception area upstairs.

His confidence faded as he opened the office door and waited for an acknowledgment.

"Take a seat, Denis." His boss finally addressed him, leaned back in his leather chair, and twiddled his thumbs.

Hamilton was overcome with panic. He didn't appreciate Allen's serious tone, and he wondered if the meeting was not for an update but rather a dismissal from the investigation.

"I need to be frank with you, Denis. I explained that I wasn't going to let you dawdle on this case, that I wanted results. Maybe it should be handed over to another team."

"We can handle it, sir."

Allen raised his hand to silence him. "Do you have any idea the pressure I'm under to get results? We're dealing with a serial killer, and we can't be seen dragging our heels any longer. My superiors are looking to me for answers, the same way I expect them from you. But you're giving me nothing, Denis! Five women! Five women have been murdered in a very small time frame, and you have no flaming results."

Panic turned to fury. Hamilton clenched his fists under the table but remained tight-lipped until he was sure he wouldn't roar at his superior. He understood the Met's desire for positive statistics and results, but he would not let his team's hard work go unnoticed.

"I'm well aware of the body count, sir," he finally replied. "And I know you're tempted to take the case from us. But tell me how it would benefit the force to pass this case on with no leads and no DNA? They'd have to start from scratch. My team know the people involved, they've done the digging into the victims' lives, and they've offered overtime." He beamed with pride for his colleagues.

"Yes, Sunday's overtime. What about that then? Didn't you have a suspect in here for questioning?"

"Yes, Mr. Dexter." Hamilton explained the details of the interview and why they had released Eric. He thought it best not to share his uneasy gut feeling toward their only suspect, and was keen to deliver only the facts at this stage.

"It's not good enough, Denis. Arrest him."

"Sir, I've clearly explained we don't have enough evidence to do that. Yes, he was in a relationship with one of the victims, and that aroused our suspicions, but there's just not enough for an arrest warrant."

"Denis, I want you to use whatever evidence or suspicions you have so far on this Dexter fellow. I'll sort out the warrant today and get back to you once I've got the go-ahead. Then while we have him in custody, we'll tear his home apart and find some damning proof."

Hamilton rolled his eyes at DCI Allen's use of the word *we*. *How interesting that the boss is part of the team now an arrest is on the cards.* However, as much as he would have loved to arrest Eric, he couldn't ignore the utter lack of evidence. Eric Dexter was not exactly a well-known celebrity, but anyone in the public eye could easily cause trouble for his team if the arrest didn't stick.

He attempted to challenge his boss. "Sir—"

"Don't you argue with me, Denis Hamilton," Allen bellowed, slamming the phone back into its dock. "We need to show the press we are making progress with this investigation. Everyone and their bloody dog knows about this investigation! We can't just sit around looking pretty. Make the arrest, Denis, before the Met has a public outcry on its hands."

The chief's statement was final, and Hamilton knew no good would come of his arguing. He nodded slowly and rose from the chair. Allen was right—they had to show the families of the victims, not just the general public, that the police force was doing everything possible to find the murderer. Besides, if his intuition about Eric was right, perhaps the warrant could help his team find the clues they were missing so far.

"Denis," Allen called out as he was just about to leave the office. "My priority today will be to obtain that arrest warrant for Mr. Eric Dexter. I want you to be ready, with reinforcements in place for backup. Brief your colleagues and ensure that everyone's singing from the same hymn sheet on this one."

Hamilton silently shut the door behind him and stomped past Betty. He wanted to rant and tell his boss, who sat comfortably behind his desk, firing orders, that his team was always ready for action.

CHAPTER THIRTY-ONE

Grace walked up the path to her psychiatrist's office, eager for the next session.

Maria opened the front door, again in an array of colour: pink, lime and lilac. Rather than being shocked by the mixed ensemble, she felt comforted by the constant brightness the woman offered.

Once upstairs, Maria gestured for Grace to take her place on the reclining chair while she busied herself with making tea in the snug alcove.

"It's lovely to see you again. How have you been this past week?" Maria asked.

"It's been a bit of a rollercoaster. I feel like I've experienced every emotion possible. I argued with my mum, and I hate it. I feel guilty because I'm always lashing out at her recently. I drank too much on the weekend—I know that. Needless to say, my boss was not impressed when I sauntered in to work looking like a tramp." She tried to laugh off the memory.

"Do you have a drinking problem?"

Grace was taken aback by the abrupt question, and she hesitated. "I don't think so. But, maybe—since my granddad died, I have been drinking more than I used to. I have grown up since my wild party days, but I do still enjoy a glass of wine or beer when I'm out with my girlfriends. Since the funeral… well, honestly, yes, I have been drinking more often, sometimes alone and not in a social environment, either. And the hangovers are the worst I've ever had."

"Do you want to talk about your grandfather today?"

"No," she answered sharply.

"Okay, that's fine. I told you, we'll take this at your pace. So, you said it's been a rollercoaster of a week. Would you care to explain further?"

"Okay... well, there's this guy at work. His name is Eric. I don't think I told you about him during my last session."

Grace spent the next twenty minutes divulging the details about Eric, Emily, and the unfortunate situation she had found herself in. She was exhausted just from reliving the events of the past two weeks, so she lifted her legs and lay back on the chair. She stared at the paintings on the wall in front of her as she drifted into a daydream.

"Hello? Grace, are you okay?" Maria called out softly.

She finally returned from her brief trance and scanned the room. Maria rose from her chair, poured a glass of water, and held it out, calling Grace's name a few more times.

"I'm so sorry, just overcome with my own thoughts there for a minute." Grace giggled nervously. "I have so much on my mind at the moment. I think talking about it all, out loud to you, just tired me out a bit. Sorry, is that normal?"

"I don't think anyone is in a position to determine what is or isn't normal. As individuals, we have to decide what we feel comfortable with in life. In my opinion, it would seem you're under a lot of pressure at the moment, so I'm not surprised your mind needs a respite. Talking things through like this will always bring your emotions to the forefront of your mind, and it can be an exhausting journey for some people. Especially if you're the type of person who is used to bottling things up," Maria said, offering a warm, reassuring smile. "Do you feel comfortable to move on?"

Grace nodded. Keen to shake off the fatigue, she sat up and crossed her legs.

"Okay, so how did you get on with the diary-writing task I set you?"

"I only wrote in it a few times because I haven't suffered much from the dreams. Except one night. But I do like the idea.

It felt good to capture everything I remembered and how I've been feeling in general," Grace explained, as she fished through her handbag for the notebook.

"Let's focus on the one episode you suffered."

She flicked through the pages and, using her early-morning scribbles as a prompt, detailed the images to Maria.

"Can you think of anything that triggered this particular nightmare?"

"No. Why?"

"I ask because, as you've only had the one nightmare since our last session, I wonder if we can try and determine what, if anything, caused it," Maria explained.

"That's interesting."

"So you're happy to continue with our sessions?"

Grace contemplated for a moment. Whilst her dreams and the lack of understanding she had of them caused her great fear, a part of her wanted to unlock the meaning behind them.

"Yes, I do want to carry on Maria," she answered confidently.

"I'm glad. Going forward I suggest you write in the diary every day, even if it's just a few sentences. Make a note of what you've done that day and how you felt; of course always include any nightmares you have. At our next session, we can identify if there is a correlation between your waking and sleeping state. We may find an indicator to what the visions mean."

"Okay, I can do that. Plus, if the dreams don't return, it's a good source to release my emotions; otherwise, they're unleashed on my mother."

"That's brilliant progress, Grace, and a great way to look at this exercise. And you're right—it may be a good outlet for when you're ready to talk about your grandfather. You can include your feelings about him too."

Grace pulled at her jumper sleeve and looked at her watch. They had run five minutes past the end of their session, and Maria hadn't stopped her talking. She gathered her coat and bag, thanked the psychiatrist, and headed for the stairs.

At the front door, Maria tapped her gently on the arm. "As we've said, let's use your diary as a tool. It will assist me, give me more of an insight, and from there, I'll be able to formulate some more ideas about the way forward for our therapy."

"Thank you, Maria. I look forward to next week."

CHAPTER THIRTY-TWO

Hamilton and Clarke waited anxiously in the car for the go-ahead signal, announcing the reinforcements' readiness to storm in. Out in the bitter cold, the Specialist Firearms Command team moved into position around Eric Dexter's apartment. They covered the front and back entrances so he couldn't attempt to escape.

Harbouring mixed emotions, Hamilton grasped the arrest warrant in his hands. DCI Allen and his contacts had unmistakably rushed through the process of obtaining the affidavit. He was thankful for the speed, yet couldn't shake the doubt that the swiftness of securing the warrant had nothing to do with his team's hard work, and everything to do with the Met's determination to keep the press on their side. Hamilton had decided Fraser would stay at the station while the arrest took place. He'd left her clear instructions to dig further into every aspect of Eric's private and professional life. He wanted to ensure he was armed with as much information as possible during the arresting interview. Morris and Wedlock sat waiting in a squad car opposite the apartment.

The last Firearms officer took his place at the bottom of the porch steps, turned to Hamilton and gestured with his hand for them to approach.

"That's our cue," he confirmed. "SCO19 are in place and awaiting our lead."

The two of them jumped from the car and signalled for their colleagues to follow suit. They all bolted up the stairs towards Eric's apartment and halted at his front door.

"Mr. Dexter! Open up. It's the police," Hamilton's voice bellowed through the wind. "If you don't open the door, we'll break it down."

He stood aside and nodded to the Specialist Firearms Officer to his left, who positioned himself with the door breach in place.

"I would guess it's too early in the morning for him to be out, so he might try and do a runner. Be on the ball," Hamilton said, pointing to his team. "Clarke and I will head straight upstairs. Morris, I want you and Wedlock to search the ground floor."

The officer made light work of cracking down the front door. Making straight for the stairs, both Hamilton and Clarke identified themselves as they climbed the steps two at a time. He noticed Eric's bed had not been slept in. With every room thoroughly checked, the duo made their way back down to the rest of the team.

"Gov! You need to get in here, now!" Wedlock shouted.

He pushed past Clarke and raced into the kitchen. Stopping suddenly, he was greeted by a pool of blood saturating the white-tiled floor. His eyes trailed the length of the body, noting the knife and bruised face. Eric Dexter was dead. Furious, Hamilton punched the door frame and stormed back into the hallway.

When Laura and her pathology team arrived at the scene, SCO19 had already left, and his team had begun processing the murder investigation. Not wanting to lose momentum, Hamilton and Clarke knocked on the neighbours' doors to determine if any of them had heard any disturbances from Eric's apartment. Most were unhelpful and explained that residents on the street liked their privacy and kept themselves to themselves. The elderly man directly opposite Eric's home, however, said he had conducted his normal neighbourhood watch duty before going to bed. He explained his neighbour had returned home the previous evening at approximately eleven thirty.

"It stuck in my head because he wasn't alone," Mr. Peters continued, and Clarke jotted down the man's version of events.

"Obviously, that's not the strange thing at all. You know that man is in and out at all times with female guests. What I did think odd last night was that he was with a man. But then I suppose you get all sorts working in the theatre, or so I've heard."

"You're positive it was a man, Mr. Peters?" Clarke questioned.

"Of course, my boy. I may be getting on a bit, but I've no problem with my eyesight. Plus, they were quite noisy, so I could definitely make out two male voices."

"Do you think you could give us a description of the other man or perhaps identify him in a line-up if need be?"

"Oh no, I'm sorry, Detective. I didn't get a good look at him. In fact, I didn't even see his face. I just knew it was a man by his voice, like I said, and his height. You know, that sort of thing."

The pair gathered as much information from Mr. Peters as possible, but considering he called himself 'neighbourhood watch', Hamilton was disappointed with the lack of specifics. They returned to Eric's apartment, which had been cordoned off as an official crime scene, and updated their colleagues.

"Well, it's something to work on," Morris said optimistically. "I wonder if they arrived in separate cars. It could be worth checking out the local CCTV when we're back at the station."

"Mr. Peters couldn't confirm. Make that your number one priority, Sharon," Hamilton replied.

"No problem, boss. While we're here, do you still want us to do a search of the property, in connection with the women's murders?"

"I don't think there's much point. From the scene in there, I think we can safely say we were wrong about Mr. Dexter. Forensics will handle everything else, and we can do a cross-check from that if need be. You two head back to the station, update Kerry, and start investigating that CCTV footage."

The sergeants turned their backs to leave the apartment, and Hamilton walked slowly into the kitchen. The pathology team worked vigorously around Eric's lifeless body heaped on the floor, and Clarke took notes while Laura dictated their findings.

"Inspector, I don't want to give you any false information, so perhaps we should wait until after the post-mortem before I give you my prognosis. I know how important this case is," Laura said.

Hamilton raised an eyebrow; he had worked with the pathologist long enough to know when she was trying to shield herself from being swamped by his questions.

"I would estimate that time of death is between midnight and four a.m., pretty much the same time frame as your last victim, Inspector. I wonder if that's intentional, significant somehow. Anyway, I really don't want to say any more to lead the investigation down the wrong path. However, I can promise you this will be my first post-mortem when I get back to the mortuary, and you're more than welcome to join me," Laura offered.

"Brilliant idea. Yes, Clarke and I will follow you there now." He paused to study her face. *What are you holding back, missy?* "I'd like the results immediately… especially as I know there's something you're not telling me."

She scrunched up her face. "Fine, you sussed me out. But you can't use anything I say here as fact until after the post-mortem. You got that?"

He nodded a bit too enthusiastically, and she gave a half smile.

"I believe the knife was plunged into Mr. Dexter's chest *after* he was killed."

CHAPTER THIRTY-THREE

News of Eric's murder spread quickly through the theatre. Actors and crew members gathered in the auditorium to share their colourful memories of their colleague and friend. Some sat alone in utter shock while others, mainly the women of the group, cried hysterically as they realised they would never spend a night with the lead actor again—in more ways than one.

Grace left them for the solitude of her office, buried her head in her hands, and sobbed uncontrollably. She regretted their last conversation had been bitter and heated after many years of friendship. She allowed herself to accept the fact that she wouldn't see Eric again; the pain erupted inside her because she couldn't remember exactly why she had been so angry with him. *I knew he was a ladies' man. Why did I take it to heart so much?* Her thoughts forced the tears to flow faster, and her shoulders shook violently.

"Knock, knock! Can I come in?" Michael jibbed as he peered round the door.

Grace lifted her head but didn't have the energy for much else. She was aware of her dishevelled appearance. Snot, tears and makeup all merged together, but she couldn't move to help herself. Michael grabbed a handful of tissues from the box on her table and crouched down to give them to her. She accepted, letting out a sad and loud sigh. Although she dabbed the tissues along her face gently, no amount of tissues could remove the grief that felt so fresh to her once again.

"I can't believe he's gone, Michael."

"I know. It's come as a shock to us all." He rested his hand on top of hers.

"But murdered! First Emily, and now Eric—it can't be true. It seems this theatre is cursed."

"Grace, don't say things like that. Perhaps there's a connection because the two of them were in a relationship. We can't ignore the obvious link. But I most definitely think this theatre is not to blame." Michael stood, perched his backside on the table, and interlocked his fingers with hers.

"What will we do, Michael? We'll have to cancel the show."

"I'm afraid we'll do no such thing, my dear. We've already lost an abundance of performance time at the beginning of the year. Do you know how much money we'll lose if we cancel more shows?"

She pulled away from him and rose from the office chair. Furious at his lack of sympathy, she walked towards the door, rubbing her hands together. "Michael, that's unforgivable. Our lead actor has been murdered, and you want to go on with the show. What will our audience think of such callous behaviour? Not to mention our actual staff members who must be going through hell. The pain they will be suffering from losing a colleague, a friend. First, Emily's life was snatched away, and we didn't give them any compassionate leave—are you seriously suggesting we ignore that yet another employee has been murdered?" Her voice rose an octave.

Michael walked towards her and placed a hand on each of her shoulders. "Grace, darling, please don't make me out to be the heartless one. I'll allow everyone to have the rest of the day off. We will of course have to do some damage limitations with the press and the tickets purchased for this evening. Don't worry, I'll take care of everything after I've sent you all home."

She was horrified at the thought of continuing as normal, but her stiff body eased, grateful that, albeit half-heartedly, Michael had taken on board her suggestion.

He continued, "However, I think you're placing your own emotions onto the rest of the staff. So it will only be the one night we close the theatre. I want work to resume as normal tomorrow, with Blake playing the lead role."

"What are you talking about?" Grace's eyes widened in shock.

"I know you had a relationship with Eric. Please don't try and deny it. I heard your confrontation on opening night. Don't worry, I didn't tell anyone. And actually, maybe you should keep that little to-do the pair of you had to yourself as well. I didn't say anything because you are a valued member of my team, and I'd hate to lose you. I had hoped it was a one-off mistake on your behalf, and from what I heard that day, it seemed unlikely to happen again. Well, I think we can safely say it definitely won't happen again."

She felt faint, reeling from Michael's revelations and his cold attitude. She threw on her coat, clutched her bag, and left the office.

"I think we should talk to the team together, Grace. Put on a unified front," he said, following her out the door.

She spun round angrily. "There is nothing unified about the way we're thinking at the moment. I'm mourning a colleague, and you're thinking about money. You're merciless, and should be ashamed of yourself."

As Grace walked through the suffocating corridor, she heard Michael call out to her. "That's show business, darling!"

****

The afternoon grew dark as black clouds grouped together, threatening to explode into a rainstorm over the quiet cemetery. Numb from the grief and alcohol, Grace couldn't feel the coldness as she sat on frosty grass next to her grandfather's grave. She unscrewed the red cap of the half-litre bottle of vodka she'd bought at the nearby newsagent and swigged back a mouthful.

The alcohol had the desired effect. The clear liquid burnt her chest as it slithered down her throat, but she welcomed its harshness because it culled her thoughts. She slumped; staring idly at nothing, thinking of nothing in particular and totally unaware of her surroundings. Her statue state lasted a short while before a blast of liveliness ran through her.

"Why? Why has death filled my life since you left me, Granddad? And not just slow sad deaths like yours, but murdah," she slurred. "Cruel individuals stealing innocent people's lives. I hate this evil world. I feel so alone and confused. What can I do to stop all this loss in my life?"

Grace gulped more vodka, fast and aggressively. The sharp taste became warm and inviting. The cemetery was lonely and quiet, as it had been during most of her visits, and she wondered if the tradition of visiting departed loved ones had declined within society.

"I hope no one forgets about me when I die. I could never forget about you, Granddad, and I promise I'll always come and visit to tell you what's going on. I hardly ever see other mourners when I'm here. It's so sad."

She sat quietly for a long time, continued to ignore the damp seeping through her clothes and the red tinge her hands had adopted. When the bottle of vodka was finally empty, she threw it opposite her grandfather's grave, rested her head on the ground, and curled up into the foetal position.

"I'm so scared, Granddad. I just want to run away and not feel the pain any more," she said weakly, and fell asleep.

****

When Grace finally woke up, her neck was stiff, but she felt warm. She was lying on a soft sofa with a fleece blanket over her. She was no longer at the cemetery, and she rushed to sit up so swiftly that her head spun from the motion. She closed her eyes, allowing the alcohol-induced dizziness to slow down, before studying her surroundings. It didn't take long to realise she was safe at home, in the living room. *How the hell did I get here? I can't remember a thing. Oh my God, did I fall asleep at the cemetery? No I obviously made it back here before passing out!* The smell of coffee disrupted her musings—she wasn't alone in the house. With the effects of the alcohol still in her system, she felt brave and ventured from the comfort of the warm blanket into the kitchen.

Grace opened the door and was greeted with a harrowing glare from her mother. She remained silent, wanting to gauge the mood and hopefully regain her memory. Saying nothing, Valerie turned her back to continue cooking. She found her mother's reaction immature and sniggered while stumbling through the room towards the fridge.

"I'm afraid you won't find any alcohol in there," Valerie said.

"I bought two bottles of wine yesterday, so I think you'll find I will."

"The wine I poured down the sink half an hour ago, you mean?"

"How dare you?" Grace snapped, slamming the fridge door with such force, it shook against the cupboard.

Valerie dropped her cooking utensils and spun round. "I found you asleep at your granddad's grave. Well, *comatose* would be a better description. There was an empty bottle of vodka near you, and don't try and deny it, Grace—I know it was yours. I rang your father, he carried you to the car and placed you on the sofa. You didn't stir once." Valerie's eyes welled up as she relived the experience. "I've not long come in from the living room. I just sat there, watching you sleep for ages. Every time I thought of my unconscious daughter lying on the ground of a public place, alone and in the dark, fear clenched my stomach, and I wanted to be sick. What if someone else found you, Grace?" Her mother slid down along the sideboard.

"This is a bit of a scene. It was just a little drink. I had some bad news at work." Embarrassed by her mother's outburst, she longed to escape the room.

"Are you listening? What if it wasn't me that found you? There is a murderer out there, killing women." Valerie finally dragged herself from the floor and moved closer to her. "I heard about Eric on the news, and when you didn't answer your mobile, I was worried about you. I rang the theatre, and Michael said you had left hours before. I knew there was only one place you would go. I just never imagined to find you in that state."

Neither of them spoke for some time. Grace desperately wanted a way out, a solution to end the depressing atmosphere growing fierce in the small kitchen. Knowing her mother could never deny her a hug, she moved forward and embraced Valerie. As the hangover began to kick in, the comfort of a hug was a welcoming one.

"I'm sorry I made you worry like that, Mum. It wasn't intentional. When I heard about Eric, the devastation took over. I should have just come home. I know that now."

Valerie pulled from the embrace and looked deep into her daughter's eyes. "Grace, I'm seriously concerned about the way you're handling everything. I understand you're grieving, more than most at the moment, and I can't pretend to know what you're going through—"

"Then don't try to! Don't start another lecture and don't pour my wine down the sink. I'm a grown woman who doesn't deserve to be treated like this!"

"You might be a grown woman, Grace, but you sure as hell are not acting like one. I thought your counselling sessions would help more, but you keep turning to the booze. I've had enough! Do you know how lucky you are? Anything could have happened to you out there this evening. Don't you care about yourself? I can't watch you do this any more."

"Then I won't stick around and force you to watch it." Her temper escalated again, and she charged through the kitchen out to the front door. The quick search for her handbag was a disappointing one.

Valerie leaned against the doorframe, her arms folded and eyebrows raised. Grace hated the knowing glint in her mother's eyes.

"You won't find your things, Grace. I've hidden them and locked the front door. There'll be no frantic escape for more alcohol tonight."

"So you're keeping me prisoner?" She looked her mother up and down, furious at the confident posture on show.

"If that's how you want to look at it, go ahead. I'm doing this for your own benefit. I don't want you to think the answer to your problems is to get drunk. You'll do something stupid or, God forbid, leave yourself vulnerable and asking for trouble. I will never be able to erase today's image of you from my mind, and I refuse to go through that again."

With no fight left in her, Grace admitted defeat and climbed the stairs to her bedroom. She knew she had to at least try to sleep off the sickly feeling that was rising in her throat. And although she could hear her mother's sobs behind her, for the second time that day, she could feel nothing but a numb sensation.

CHAPTER THIRTY-FOUR

The two detectives strode through the incident room, eager to update their colleagues on Eric's post-mortem. The team stopped what they were doing immediately and, while Clarke carried out his usual task of updating the board, Hamilton relayed the details.

"Laura confirmed that Dexter's knife wound was not the cause of death; the killer did in fact stab him once he was already dead. And not with much force either."

"So you think we already have a copycat killer on our hands, gov?" Morris called out from where she sat behind her computer.

"Mmm… I don't know about a copycat, Sharon. We have to remember that Dexter had connections with the other victims. I know I was an advocator of his guilt, but I'm prepared to hold my hands up and say my gut instinct may have been wrong this time. We need to dissect this one carefully. Lewis, you go over the other aspects of Laura's report."

Clarke returned the black marker to the board and faced the team. "Blunt-force trauma to the head is what killed Eric Dexter. Pathology have confirmed the glass object was hefty and thick; fragments remained in the victim's skull, so if we can find the murder weapon, Laura will be able to match it."

"There was nothing at the scene. Forensics conducted a thorough search," Wedlock offered.

"I know, Les, but that's not to say the killer didn't take it with him." Clarke glimpsed back at his notepad and recovered his train of thought. "Okay, what we do know is that the murderer left the knife impaled in Dexter's chest. A knife that was taken from his own kitchen, and the incisions do not match the other victims' wounds. This took place in his home with no sign of forced entry, and from his defensive wounds, we know he put up a fight. It's likely that our killer has some contusions of his own. Lastly, we can't ignore that he's male; so the dissimilarities with this victim are apparent."

The team digested all the information before firing ideas amongst each other. While Morris stuck with her copycat theory, believing it was someone who had cobbled together information from the media, Fraser suggested that they were still looking for the same killer, and that Eric had been the connecting factor between the dead women.

"These could have been rage killings," she explained. "All the women were linked to Eric in some way and our murderer was jealous. Perhaps he wanted them for himself and was livid that he couldn't have them. Then when he discovered Eric could, he saw red. But this time, he came across some difficulties. Maybe he's not as strong or as tall as Eric, hence the struggle between them. The use of a glass object could have been used in panic, but he wanted everyone to know it was him, so he still struck the knife into his chest anyway."

Hamilton nodded at the sergeant's suggestion. "Kerry, it looks like you're on the same wavelength as us. It's exactly what Lewis and I surmised during the car journey over here. Also, I'm pleased to say that my competent partner has left the best nugget of information for me to share with you."

Clarke sniggered, shaking his head, and Hamilton savoured the moment. Smirking in silence, he watched the team waiting eagerly for him to continue. "Our killer left his DNA all over this crime scene. It's in the process of being checked against the database right now. If he's got form, we'll have him. Finally, some concrete evidence that he murdered Dexter, and possibly our other five victims."

CHAPTER THIRTY-FIVE

Grace's hands trembled as she reached for the glass of water on her bedside table. She hadn't seen her mother since the altercation about the locked front door, so she knew Valerie had slipped in undetected during the night to leave the drink for her. Overjoyed the feeling to throw up was not bubbling in her stomach, she retrieved the diary from under her pillow to capture all she could remember about what had woken her.

Early hours of Friday morning – I'm hungover!
This nightmare was the worst; it was more vivid. More real somehow. I feel sick inside, and not from the drink. It was cold and dark, and I was alone. This time there was blood. Lots of blood, everywhere. But what I can't forget was how it gushed down her face.

Grace stopped writing to take another sip of water, trying desperately to control her shivering hands. She wiped her eyes vigorously, wanting to force herself away from the nightmare, to feel safe in her bedroom. But she knew she had to concentrate long enough to write it all down. She had to do it for Maria. She squinted as she picked up the pen again.

It was a dead woman's face. Her body was motionless and naked, covered in blood. But that's all I can see clearly and, actually, even as I write, the image is fading. It's becoming distant. Like they're pulling away from me and I can't hold on to them. Fucking hell, there's no way I can go back to sleep now. I thought yesterday's drink would help me. Save me even. But it's made me feel worse. I can't think straight right now, and I can't be sure if that's because of the dream or the hangover. It's not just the nightmares I want the alcohol to rescue me from. I want it to help me forget my life too. Eric is dead. Shit! I can't believe I just wrote that. He's dead. Murdered like Emily. And Michelle. And Kate. Maybe like me too if Mum hadn't found me first in the cemetery. There has to be a connection!!! Christ, my tongue feels enormous, and dry… maybe I will throw up. This hangover is pure evil. It's building in momentum. What did I drink? Too bloody much, whatever it was. It's probably a blessing that Mum bolted me in last night. I'm asking for trouble. But sometimes I can't help myself, it blocks the pain. For a few hours anyway, I forget how much I'm hurting. It numbs the aching.

I can't believe I'll never see Eric's perfect face again.

This has to stop. I'll talk to Mum and to Maria. I'll get some help.

Grace lowered her knees, where she had been resting the diary, and dropped the book onto the bed. She stared into space for a few moments, thoughts of the loved ones she'd lost ran through her mind. *Are there clues that I can find a connection to?* She surveyed the room, spotted her bag hanging on the door handle, and was overjoyed her mum had returned it. She threw off the covers, bounced across the room, and returned to the warmth of her duvet with her handbag. Once she'd retrieved her iPhone, she searched through the contacts list, stopping at Michael's name and selected the text message option.

Michael, I'm sorry, but I won't be coming in to work today. You may be right, the team might not be affected by all this tragedy, but I am. I need to grieve for my friend. Feel free to take it out of my holiday leave, I know I have plenty. I'll be in contact next week. Grace.

Once the text was sent, she held down the power button to switch off the phone. Grace had decided she didn't want to be disturbed, and despite it being only five in the morning, she wrapped herself in the fluffy white robe draped at the bottom of her bed and switched on her laptop. Somewhere deep inside, a part of her wasn't ready to give in to the alcohol and pity, and that spurred her on. She wanted to discover what had really happened to her friends and why they had been murdered.

****

Valerie almost dropped the mug of tea after she opened the bedroom door and absorbed the sight before her. Her daughter energetically worked over her laptop, oblivious to her presence. Grace's brunette locks were loose and wild; they had evidently been pulled through by her fingers quite a few times. The shadows dulling her skin gave a clue to her lack of sleep, but her eyes were wide and frantic. Discarded papers were tossed all over the floor, some with Grace's handwriting on them, others obviously printed from the Internet. Without her glasses, Valerie couldn't read the information on them.

As she walked farther in the room, it became clear that the paperwork wasn't confined to the floor—it was spread out over the desk and bed. Grace continued to tap away, ignoring Valerie's attempts to gain her attention. Printouts were highlighted in different sections, an array of coloured pens lay on the desk without lids, and sticky notes had been placed all over the wall above the laptop. She had never witnessed such chaos in her daughter's room. It wasn't like Grace to work in such a disorganised mess, and Valerie's already-growing concern for her daughter made her shudder at the scene.

"What are you doing?"

Valerie was startled by the sound of Grace's voice, not realising she had stopped typing. "Well, I was going to ask you the same question, dear."

Eyeing her daughter suspiciously, she placed the mug of tea on a stack of papers.

Grace frowned, removed the mug from where her mother had put it and placed it on the floor. "I'm doing some research, Mum. I think I can help my friends who were brutally killed."

"How can you, love? I'm so worried about you. Should I call for the doctor?" She was in turmoil, thinking about whom she could ask for help.

"I don't need a doctor! I can find their killer. I can help the police catch this evil monster." Grace's excited eyes widened as she collected pages and shoved them into Valerie's hands.

"These nightmares I'm having could be some form of psychic ability, Mum. At first, I thought they could be premonitions, but I've realised that's foreseeing the future. I've dreamt of dead bodies, so that obviously can't be the case. But what if I'm having clairvoyant visions? Some research even suggests that in our dreaming state, we're more open to communication from the dead. As I'm finding it difficult to piece the memories of all of them together, this could be a possibility. But I need to do some more research. Did you want something?" Grace spoke so quickly that it took Valerie a few moments to register all the information.

She stood gawking at her daughter in silence. Her anxiety hit a new high as she struggled to comprehend Grace's state of mind. Together, they had watched many TV programmes about people claiming to be psychic, or to possess the ability to talk with dead people, but neither of them had believed it. She thought of times when the two of them had chuckled at the outrageousness of these people's claims, adamant it was all concocted for TV entertainment. She was dumbfounded that Grace had come to not only believe it, but to think it was something she could do. *Maybe the loss of her granddad has affected her much more than I realised.*

"Mum! Seriously, I'm busy. Can I help you with something?" Grace's aggressive tone snapped her from her thoughts.

"I'm just a bit shocked, if I'm honest, darling. I thought we both felt the same about all this nonsense."

"That's the thing, I don't think it's nonsense at all any more. I know we've both said you can never be sure if those people are just out to make money, but now it's happening to me, I can understand it. All this information on the Internet is brilliant too,

Mum. You should read it. There are groups of people, including scientists, that have conducted assessments into the reality of clairvoyance, mediums, and other psychic abilities. Also the significance of different dreams or nightmares and the meanings behind them."

"Well, that is interesting," Valerie said with a fake smile. "But shouldn't you be at work? I'm sure Michael is worried about you. It's ten a.m."

"Don't be silly; I sent him a message when I woke up, about five hours ago. That's when I knew I could help them. I've been delving into all this ever since. I know now that my visions are a sign that I'm supposed to do something, that I have to help. Please, Mum, just let me get on." Grace's eyes bulged, filled with an intensity Valerie had never witnessed before.

She feared that any disagreement could alter her daughter's mood further and create an argument between them, so she decided not to exacerbate the situation. She smiled sweetly and wished Grace luck with the research.

"Darling, I'll be downstairs if you need me, or if you want to have a chat about anything you find out, okay?" she called from the bedroom door.

Apprehension seeped through her mind as she watched Grace work between her laptop and notebooks in a frenzy. Although she was glad her daughter had no interest in reaching for the wine bottle, she couldn't help but worry that her attraction to paranormal activities was just another unhealthy distraction.

Grace didn't take her eyes from her work and called out, "It's fine, Mum. I have a session with Maria this evening. I'm going to discuss it all with her."

With a deep sorrowful feeling, Valerie shut the door on her daughter.

CHAPTER THIRTY-SIX

Maria sensed a change in Grace's mood immediately and was eager to find out why. Regardless of the fact that they had conducted only two sessions together, they had clearly formed a close bond. She could tell her patient was excited to discuss something with her, which made her feel proud of the progress that was taking place. She couldn't help but smile to herself as she watched Grace like an eager puppy on the reclining chair, desperate to start their session. But Maria was a lady of routine. In her twenty-odd years as a psychiatrist, she'd come to understand the importance of patience in these situations and didn't want to rush anything. She wanted to control the setting and conjure a calmer atmosphere, and a calmer Grace. Maria set about her normal routine of boiling the kettle—she believed that a warm cup of tea could bring tranquility to any scenario.

"I've really been looking forward to today's session," Grace blurted out, obviously unable to sit in silence any longer.

Maria turned and gave her usual warm smile but continued making the tea instead of indulging Grace in discussion. She wanted to fully examine Grace's mood, and she always preferred to receive information without asking too many questions, as much as she sometimes wanted to.

"I think I finally understand why I've been having these nightmares, and I need your help."

"Of course. You know that's what I'm here for: to help you."

As Maria sipped her tea, Grace divulged the day's activity of research. Hearing her patient talk so enthusiastically and sound so positive about her ideas gave Maria a pleasant feeling. However, Grace had left her cup of tea untouched on the table—a first for her.

"I know I don't have diary entries from when the ordeals began, but I thought back to when I suffered the most awful ones. There was the time after I slept with Eric, and then again when I had that argument with him on opening night. It's made me wonder now if those dreams were warning me that Eric was the next victim. What do you think, Maria?"

"I believe that exploring the inner workings of our minds can uncover a lot. The brain is an intricate organ that determines what we remember, what we process on a day-to-day basis, and then how we decipher that information in order to just make it through the day. And each individual does these tasks and copes with these things differently. It's an amazing thing. I haven't studied premonitions or clairvoyance, so unfortunately, I can't comment on that, but there may be another way I can help. If you're open to it."

Grace clapped her hands together in excitement. "Yes, I thought the same. It was foolish of me to not think of it sooner really, and it wasn't until today during my research that I suddenly remembered the details on your business card. You're a clinical hypnotherapist!"

"That's correct." Maria couldn't contain her smile as she watched the excitement pour over Grace's face. "It could definitely be an avenue we discuss and consider for your future sessions, as you've described a reoccurring theme to your dreams that's affecting your everyday life. Hypnotherapy may be able to help us unmask the true meaning behind them, because the process takes us into our subconscious minds, while having the benefit of being awake and alert."

"Please, Maria, I want to do it as soon as possible," Grace said as she shuffled to the edge of her seat, hunger in her eyes. "Like you said, it is affecting my everyday life. I called in sick at work today, and that's very unlike me. The disturbed sleep is gruelling. But the most frustrating thing is not being able to fully remember the images that are causing me to feel such panic when I wake up. If these are some form of psychic visions, then I have to be able to help myself and the police. I've been through so much death and pain lately, I so badly want to turn these horrific nightmares into something positive. And even if there is absolutely no connection, and they're just a cruel coincidence, I have to uncover them so I can rid myself of them. I have to move on." Grace caught the teardrop on her finger before it slipped off her chin.

Maria admired the young woman's determination, and resolved that she would use her expertise to help Grace unmask the internal demons.

****

On the bus journey home, Grace was eager to share her excitement and could think of only one person to contact. She reached into her bag for her phone, opened WhatsApp, and brought up the previous conversation with Natasha. Pleased to see her friend's status was 'online', she began typing.

Grace: Hey hon x

Natasha: Hey sweetie! What's up? X

Grace: I'm on the way home, fancy popping round? X

Natasha: I'm about five mins from The Oak, meet you there? X

Grace: I really don't feel like drinking. Any chance you could ditch a night in the pub and come round for a cuppa. I'd love to chat. X

Natasha: Tea!! On a Friday night???? OK, who is this and what have you done with my mate? X

She laughed at her friend's comment and was glad the bus wasn't packed, although it didn't stop the nosey elderly lady in front of her from spinning round for a look.

Grace: I'm here, it's me, lol! Just decided to give the drinking a break for a while. I've got a lot going on and need a clear head. X

Natasha: OK, no worries chick. Can't meet you though as I've already promised to have a drink with Nicky. X

Grace: Nicky? I thought it was Ben? X

Natasha: That was so last week sweetie, LOL. Slightly complicated as they're friends, but I'll get my kicks where I can. Men have no problem doing it to us, you know that. It's sexist!! How dare they think they can outsmart us women in the sex games? I'll show them LOL. #RantOver x

Grace sighed. She hated the way her friend could bounce from one man to the next, never settling down. Granted, she wasn't in a loving relationship herself, but she had wanted to be with Eric—she realised that now more than ever. She had been so angry at him for playing the field, but was now worried her dear friend was going down the same route. She began typing, determined to reprimand Natasha's behaviour and advise her not to play silly games. To find true love. But she quickly deleted the message—she knew Natasha wouldn't appreciate her attitude on the subject. And deep down, Grace felt stupid spouting about romance.

Grace: Be careful out there, Tash. There's some freaks on the street xx
Natasha: Don't worry about me. I can take care of myself, I'm hard as nails, lol. Catch up soon… I promise!!! X

She awkwardly gathered her belongings together and rushed to press the bell. Deep in her conversation with Natasha, she had almost missed her stop. The elderly lady tutted at the commotion Grace made in her haste to exit the bus, so she gave her a sarcastic wave as the bus pulled away from its stop.

The evening had descended into darkness. Clinging her handbag, she picked up the pace. It was only a ten-minute walk from the bus stop to her house, but panic set in. She was sure she could hear footsteps behind her, but every time she looked over her shoulder, no one was there. Her mind filled with the memories of when she had run from the imaginary footsteps before—and fallen straight into Eric's arms. Sadness washed over her. *I wish he were here now.*

The sound of a car rumbled nearby. As the engine drew closer, a black sports car crawled along the road. Its tinted windows hid whoever was inside, and Grace was tempted to take flight. Her feet were stubborn and stopped walking when the car came to a halt next to her. She held her breath, staring at the lavish, but unfamiliar, Subaru. *Run, god damn it, woman! Home is just around the corner. Run!*

The passenger's door swung open. A white bald man leaned out against the car door and spoke with a strong cockney accent.

"Here, treacle! You couldn't tell us how to get to Wembley Stadium, could 'ya? We're gonna miss the match at this rate."

Relieved no one was about to drag her kicking and screaming into the car, she exhaled deeply but felt faint. She couldn't form the words to answer. The heavily built man moved swiftly from the car to Grace's side and held her, placing both hands on her arms.

"You all right, love? You're as pale as a flipping ghost. I didn't mean to scare 'ya."

She narrowed her eyes and shook her head in an attempt to focus on him. When she finally did, she couldn't help but smile shyly at the warmth of his kind hands gently holding her steady.

"How embarrassing. I'm so sorry," she finally replied and broke free from his grasp. "I guess I got a little spooked. You want to turn around and follow the road back the way you came, then take a right. You'll see loads of signs from there."

He frowned, obviously confused by Grace's sudden outburst of words. She couldn't contain the giggles, feeling light-headed and foolish. "The directions to Wembley. So you don't miss the match," she said with a smile.

"Ha! Flipping heck, I didn't even think you'd heard me talking to 'ya. You still look a bit dazed. Are you sure you'll be all right?" he asked.

"Thank you for the concern, but I'll be fine. Just don't get many flashy cars on these roads. I got a bit nervous."

He winked, and Grace watched as the friendly stranger returned to the car. The driver was clearly impatient, as he sped off the second the passenger's door shut. As she slowly continued on her journey home, she cursed herself for being so absurd. *Seriously? You were telling yourself to run away from someone asking for directions!* Mounting the stairs to her front door, she fiddled in her pocket for the keys, and felt compelled to turn and scan the dark street. It was silent, except for the sound of her deep panting. Regardless of feeling foolish just moments before, she was certain that someone was watching her from the shadows.

CHAPTER THIRTY-SEVEN

Hamilton's thoughts were fixed firmly on his wife. He couldn't ignore the fact that he had neglected her since before Christmas, and the guilt was eating away at him. As important as she was to him, this murder investigation had a way of creeping into his mind just as often as she did. But it was the case that always won. He clenched his fists in frustration at his personal and professional life. He had become a failure in both roles.

The mountain of paperwork on his office desk had grown since the previous day, but he ignored it and thought about his six years on the murder investigation team. Mostly, he reflected on the number of families that had received the devastating news of losing a loved one. He hated being part of that—it never got easier. In the space of a few months, his team had delivered those life-changing words to five families. The anger boiled inside when he thought of his beautiful wife walking around London, carefree in the knowledge that her husband caught the bad guys. Well, that was what she believed—except he was failing to live up to her glorified image of him. *Who's to say she's safe from the scum of this world?*

Hamilton was on the brink of lashing out. His body filled with impatient energy, he paced the office floor. His eyes focused on the odd green shade of the carpet as he walked. He could never fathom why other teams involved with cases such as this one would not treat them as top priority. Too much time was being wasted waiting for DNA results, and it enraged him. Understanding that every crime deserved thorough attention, he wondered if he was alone in expecting a degree of urgency when it came to taking a serial killer off the streets.

The office door burst open, and Hamilton was snatched away from his personal torments.

"Gov! Laura's on line two, waiting for you," Clarke said, slightly out of breath. "Sorry I didn't knock, but I know it's the call we've been waiting for."

Hamilton waved away the apology. "Why didn't she phone my direct line? I think I've been waiting long enough for the damn call."

Clarke shrugged, a confused expression on his face. Even Hamilton wondered why he was questioning the logic of the phone call rather than actually answering it. He scooted around the table and lifted the receiver to his ear.

"Laura, what can you tell me? Let it be good news."

"I'm happy to say it is, Denis. We've matched the DNA, I've just finished the complete report for you."

Hamilton punched the air in jubilation. Clarke raised his eyebrows, obviously expecting information immediately, but was ignored by his partner.

"Bloody hell, yes! Send that report to me immediately. You're a star, Laura! Thanks."

Clarke hopped impatiently from one foot to the other. "Come on, gov, this is killing me."

"We've got him, Lewis!" He practically skipped out of his office, excitedly making his way into the incident room. "I need to read over the report and show it to DCI Allen so he can request an arrest warrant. I hope we don't have to wait too bloody long for it to come through. But we've got our murderer. We've got him with full bloody proof DNA evidence this time."

CHAPTER THIRTY-EIGHT

The shrill of the phone roused Clarke from his snooze. He glanced at his alarm clock: 7:00 a.m. He did not appreciate the early weekend call when he was not on a shift. He grabbed the phone, intent on sharing his frustration.

"Rise and shine, Lewis," a cheery voice said before he had the chance to vent.

"Who the hell is this?"

"Your boss!"

Clarke cringed. "Sorry, gov, I didn't recognise your voice."

"And didn't bother to check your caller ID before answering the phone, either, apparently. Never mind, I can tell why you're pissed off, so apologies for the early wake-up call. But it's time to get yourself in gear."

"The arrest warrant has come through?"

"Not yet, you know everything official works at a snail's pace. The DCI is hopeful we'll have it by this afternoon, though I'm not holding my breath."

"So what's with the call at the crack of dawn on a Saturday?"

"We still have other avenues to cover, Lewis. I'll be outside your front door at nine a.m. Be ready," Hamilton said, and hung up.

Clarke stared at the phone and grumbled at its abrupt end. He slammed the phone on the nightstand, pulled the covers up to his neck, and snuggled back down into his warm bed. *Be ready for nine, and he calls me at seven, jheeze! What's wrong with these early-bird types?*

****

The formal black dress and blazer hung on her wardrobe door, and Grace felt distraught to be reaching for the outfit again so soon. She considered whether she could actually face another funeral, another goodbye to someone she cared about. Regret darkened the morning as she thought about the weeks leading up to Eric's death. Her decisions and his reactions had ruined their friendship, but she knew that in time, they would have made amends. She would have forgiven him. Feelings like hers didn't just vanish, and he was too important to not be part of her life. She dressed in her mourning suit and sobbed because it was too late to say sorry.

A knock on the bedroom door pulled her back into the present moment, though her eyes refused to dry. Valerie walked gingerly into the room then scooped Grace up into a loving embrace. Her tears were a steady stream of sadness falling down her face. She inhaled deeply and pulled away from her mother.

"Why are you in your suit Mum?" she asked, frowning.

"I'm coming with you, dear," Valerie replied, as she reached over and wiped the trickle of tears on Grace's cheeks. "You've suffered so much sadness these past few months; there's no way I could let you do this alone."

She smiled and hugged her mother. After they finally separated, Grace finished getting ready, and Valerie sat on the bed, watching her in silence.

They drove to the cemetery in Valerie's car, and Grace itched to fill the silence between them. She hadn't considered how another funeral would affect her mother. Desperate for conversation, she told her mother about Maria's hypnotherapy expertise and their suggestion to try to unmask her own nightmares.

"Is that safe, sweetheart? I am so worried about you," Valerie finally spoke.

"Please don't be, Mum. I have spent a lot of time researching hypnotherapy, and it's actually a very common thing to do with people suffering from recurring dreams like mine. Plus, Maria is at the top of her game in this field. I did a quick Google search on her too." She quickly squeezed her mother's hand.

"I'm glad you've looked into it then. It's best to have all the information."

She could read her mother like a book, and although Valerie hadn't said it, Grace knew she did not agree with the plan. Thankfully, her mother didn't start an argument before the funeral, and she was glad that during the remainder of the journey, Valerie listened without interruption.

As they pulled into the small car park of the crematorium, Grace worried that Eric's family hadn't appreciated the sheer number of friends, colleagues, and even acquaintances who would be paying their respects. She was eager to pass on her condolences, and once the car was parked, Grace marched confidently over to the chapel without waiting for her mother. Her conviction quickly faded when she was greeted by a weak Mr. and Mrs. Dexter crumbling into each other's arms. She managed to hug Eric's mother and shake his father's hand before swiftly returning to Valerie, who was still waiting by the car.

"Oh, wow, that was just awful. To witness them in such a state, I felt like I was intruding." Grace cried and clung to her mother for a few minutes. "I thought I could introduce myself, tell them what good friends Eric and I were and what a fantastic job he did at the theatre. But when I actually saw their faces... I thought I was going to break down and cry right in front of them. How awful of me."

"Darling, don't be so hard on yourself. I can only imagine the pain one feels after the loss of a child, at any age. Unbearable. I'm sure they'll understand his friends and colleagues feeling devastated, as well as a little awkward. Don't beat yourself up for being emotional." Valerie wrapped her arm around Grace's waist for support.

As they joined a group of mourners attempting to enter the crematorium, she noticed the detectives she'd met before, DI Hamilton and DS Clarke, walk up beside them.

"Hello, Inspector, I didn't realise you attended the funerals."

"My condolences, Miss Murphy. This must be a difficult day for you," Hamilton said. "We always ensure a member of our team attends the funeral of a murder victim. We won't stay long or outstay our welcome, but we do like to let the families know we're here for support." He lowered his voice when he uttered "murder victim," and Grace was impressed with his empathy.

"I notice not all of your colleagues are here today." The shorter of the duo, Clarke, voiced his opinion.

She got a strange feeling from him—he didn't appear kind and genuine like his partner.

"Sadly, they can't be. The theatre world isn't a nine-to-five, Monday-to-Friday job, but it'll be working on fewer numbers. I'd imagine most of the understudies will take over today so our main actors can attend," Grace answered, pointing to a few of her cast members having a sneaky cigarette. "Michael's probably remained back at the theatre, holding the fort."

"You mean you don't know that for sure? Aren't you the assistant director?" Clarke retorted.

"I've had to take a few days off, Detective, so no, I haven't spoken to him directly. It's the way we work, though. He attended Emily's funeral, and I oversaw the production. One of us must be on-site at all times."

Hamilton's smile caught her attention. "A very efficient setup, Miss Murphy. I'm sure the time away from work will be beneficial during your grieving period."

"Thank you, Inspector. I must go. It would seem my mother's gone ahead without me," Grace said before she negotiated her way through the crowd, and walked into the entrance of the crematorium.

CHAPTER THIRTY-NINE

"Lewis, we've got the arrest warrant! Sort out our backup immediately," Hamilton yelled energetically.

A buzz of excitement filled the incident room. Whoops and cheers from his team burst through the air. Clarke rushed from the information board to his desk, scooped up the phone, and made the call to SCO19, requesting their assistance urgently. Hamilton paused, waiting for his partner. He didn't want to spend precious moments going over their plan of attack twice.

"Thanks, Lewis. Now, all of you, listen up. I've just left the chief, and he's adamant that we work in two teams on this arrest," Hamilton explained. "One team to the suspect's place of work and the other team to his home. Allen's insistent that this time no mistakes or mishaps occur which could make our team look incompetent. Understand?"

Members of the team nodded or grunted their compliance. Hamilton drummed his fingers on the desk, anxious and frustrated that they were again waiting around. He glanced at his watch.

"Given the time of day, I'm confident our guy will still be at work. Lewis and I will head up that team. Les, Kerry, and Sharon, I want you to take a smaller team to the house, and even if he's not there, I want you to search the property immediately."

The trio looked confident, which filled him with an assurance of their capability. But he suppressed a snigger when the two female sergeants high-fived each other. He was thrilled with their zest for the impending task ahead of them, and would have hated to make them feel as if he were laughing at them. Hamilton explained that communication between them all was paramount, and they vowed to stay in touch with him at all times.

"We're really going to get this son of a bitch, aren't we, boss?" Wedlock said, his foot tapping repeatedly, and Hamilton knew everyone was eager to get going.

"This time, we can be sure. We've covered all our bases; he's not getting away."

The bubbling tension was too much pressure for him. Everyone needed to be moving, ready and in place for when their backup arrived.

"Right, team, we've got a knife-wielding maniac on our hands. Let's suit up."

****

Grace hadn't prepared herself for the emotional speeches that were given by Eric's family and childhood friends. She assumed, as it wasn't taking place in a church, there wouldn't be much memory sharing. Reeling in the sentiment of their personal stories, she asked Valerie to drive her to the theatre after the funeral. She felt she was being selfish to her colleagues, especially to Michael, by leaving them in the lurch during such a difficult time.

"Are you sure you're ready to face work right now, sweetie? That was a very moving service, but it was also quite draining. Your state of mind has been up and down the past few days. Well, months really. Maybe you should come home with me and have a rest."

She could see the depth of concern in her mother's eyes. Valerie was sensitive, and the last thing Grace wanted was a quarrel, not when her mother was being so considerate towards her.

"Mum, I love you, but please don't fuss over me so much. I'm not going back to work exactly. I just want to pop in and see how the performance is progressing. It will give me a chance to tell the crew about Eric's service, and I'd like to find out how Michael is. I'll be fine, I promise."

After a light-hearted debate, which Grace knew her mother could never win, Valerie reluctantly gave in to her request and drove into Central London.

Once at the theatre, Grace had only made it as far as the office corridor before she heard a commotion coming from the auditorium. She ran onto the stage, shocked to be greeted by men wielding weapons and rushing around. Voices bellowed around her, but she couldn't understand what was being said. It was loud and confusing, and she struggled to focus on one single thing. There were screams, loud bangs, and people shoving each other. She looked in every direction, desperate for an answer. Her gaze stopped on a familiar face, and she pushed violently through her trembling colleagues.

"Detective Inspector Hamilton! Tell me what the hell is going on here," Grace demanded.

But before he had a chance to explain, a message crackled through the radio that hung from his stab vest. Again, Grace couldn't make out everything that was said, but she definitely caught "suspect has been seized in his office." The two detectives gave no indication as to the reason for their intrusion, but just raced past her. Determined not to miss any vital information, she sped off in hot pursuit.

Hamilton and Clarke stormed into Michael's office as Grace caught up with them. Her boss sat calmly behind his desk, and that calmness washed over her too. *They must have made a terrible mistake.* Two burly men who resembled bodyguards stood on either side of Michael while another manned the door and attempted to stop her entrance. Hamilton, the considerate detective, waved his hand, and the brute allowed her into the room. Almost as if he had waited for her, Hamilton gave her a quick glance before addressing her superior.

"Michael Sparks, I am arresting you on the suspicion of the murder of Eric Dexter."

"What the fuck?" Grace screamed, unable to control herself.

The men in the room ignored her, and Hamilton continued to read Michael his rights as Clarke cuffed him. That calm feeling quickly vanished as she watched in horror while the men in stab vests, guns placed on their hips, dragged Michael to his feet and escorted him from the office. Michael's head remained high, but he refused to look in her direction.

"Take him to the station, boys. We'll be right behind you," Hamilton grunted.

Grace stumbled. She placed her hand out to steady herself and perched on the desk as the inspector explained they had DNA evidence against Michael, and were confident with the arrest she had just witnessed. She felt queasy as he spoke, unable to absorb the information.

"This can't be real. I only popped in to tell Michael about the funeral. Now you want me to believe it was actually him who killed Eric? No, I won't believe that But he didn't even say anything. Didn't deny it, argue against what you said. He just walked out casually. Why didn't he tell you that you're wrong? Why didn't he defend himself?" Grace rambled in a muddled haze.

But the inspector ignored her questions. "I'm sure it has come as a shock, Miss Murphy. I hope you understand that you'll need to escort everyone from the premises."

"What? No, I don't understand. Why?"

"We have a warrant to search the theatre. Everyone needs to leave immediately. A small team will stay behind to ensure nothing is tampered with. DS Clarke and I must get back to the station straight away, so please, can you cooperate with our team and get your staff out of the building?"

Grace nodded, unsure she could rely on herself to construct a sentence. The two detectives left the office, and she slumped to the ground, cross-legged. *I trusted Michael. We all trusted Michael. He is our boss and our friend. When granddad died, he was so patient and understanding. How can this be true? It can't be.* Frustrated by her conflicting thoughts, she took a few deep breaths and summoned the energy to return to the stage. The scene was manic, and everyone looked to her for answers—answers she wasn't sure she could give.

"What the hell just happened back there, Grace? These guys wouldn't let any of us leave the auditorium. Actually, they're still saying we can't." Aaron, the sound assistant, jumped at her first with the questions.

She stared off into the distance, her head dizzy from everything that had happened already. Her lack of answers prompted Aaron to step forward and nudge her shoulder.

"Erm… sorry." She shook her head, hoping it would clear her mind. "I might as well tell you all now because I'm sure the press is going to have a field day with this… Michael was just arrested for Eric's murder."

"What?"

"No way, that can't be true."

"I always thought there was something off about him."

"He wouldn't have done that. This theatre is all he cares about."

Grace couldn't tell who had said what—too many voices and opinions that she was not ready to deal with. She held both her hands up, silencing them all.

"That's all I know, and frankly, I'm not in the mood to start gossip and rumours. You're allowed to collect your belongings from the green room or your lockers, but the police will escort you to make sure you don't touch anything else. Then we all must leave the theatre."

"Excuse me, we have a performance tonight," Blake cried out.

"At a theatre where the managing director was just arrested in front of us all. For murdering the lead actor," Aaron's reply was stained with sarcasm.

She squeezed her eyes shut, unable to deal with the dramatic personalities in front of her, and rubbed her temples to ease the pressure.

"Please just get your things and leave." Grace glared at them now. "There'll be no performance tonight or any night in the near future, I'm sure. I'll contact Michael's boss, update him on the current situation, and request he call you all personally to let you know where you stand."

"Has no one ever heard of innocent until proven guilty? He could be out in a few hours, demanding an apology."

"That may be the case, Blake, but for now, the police have a search warrant. And I'm not entirely sure, but I think the theatre just became a place of interest to them. There will be no performance tonight. I'm going home. I suggest you all do the same." Grace ended the conversation, despite the grunts and chatter in her wake.

Before leaving the theatre, she told a policeman, who seemed to be in charge of the situation, where everyone would need to be escorted to in order to collect their personal belongings. He said he was happy to continue without her assistance and permitted her to leave the building. As she stepped onto the street, the bright daylight made her squint. The exhausting events of the day had taken their toll, making it feel as though it should have been midnight, not only two in the afternoon. She debated if she could actually go straight home and share the news, fretting it would only add to Valerie's growing concern for her. *No, I don't have the energy to deal with my mother's neurotic behaviour.* Grace understood it came from a place of love, but she also knew being locked in the house was something she could not deal with.

Without thinking, her feet automatically walked away from the theatre and underground station. Even on a bright afternoon, the lights and sounds from Soho's bars and restaurants were difficult to ignore. She chose somewhere she had never visited before. A place where no one would recognise her and engage her in conversation. A place where she couldn't be distracted from her ultimate goal: to get uncontrollably drunk.

CHAPTER FORTY

When Hamilton and Clarke arrived at the station, Michael's solicitor had already been contacted. The desk sergeant explained that he had read Mr. Sparks his rights and that Michael had insisted on his own representation being present during the interview. Luckily, they didn't have to wait long; thirty minutes later, the man's solicitor, Miss Holten, arrived from Forde and Partners, demanding to see her client. Feeling smug and overjoyed with the arrest, Hamilton granted her a ten-minute conference with the suspect.

Once they were together in Interview Room One, Clarke set up the recording machine and gave the obligatory information: time, date, and names of those present. Hamilton stared at Michael, silent and stern-faced. After all his years of policing, he had a certain way of discovering people's tricks and tells. He liked to use the moments before an interview to gauge the suspect's character. Michael was clearly not intimidated by Hamilton's glare. A grin was fixed firmly on the man's face, and his eyes bored back into Hamilton's.

He's an arrogant bastard, then. The tension intensified quickly.

"Mr. Sparks, do you understand the charges against you?" Hamilton finally asked.

Michael exchanged glances with his solicitor before replying. "No comment."

"Where were you the night of February ninth, Mr. Sparks?"

"No comment."

"We found your DNA at the murder scene and on the victim, Mr. Eric Dexter," he continued.

Michael hesitated while Miss Holten jotted down notes on her notepad.

"No comment."

"You see, Mr. Sparks, you can say 'no comment' as many times as you like. I'm sure that's what your solicitor here has advised you to do. But let me just share with you what I'm thinking. If you aren't willing to cooperate with us or give yourself an alibi for the time of the murder, it makes you look guilty, like you're holding something back from us. It really is as simple as that." Hamilton raised his eyebrows and leaned back into this chair.

The room descended into a frustrating silence, except for the humming noise from the recording machine.

Hamilton jumped forward and caught everyone off-guard. He pointed his finger at Michael and smiled calmly. "I mentioned your DNA was found on the murder victim, didn't I?"

The atmosphere in the room shifted. Michael was losing his composure. His nostrils flared, and he clenched his jaw. Hamilton felt triumphant.

The solicitor looked uncomfortable, twiddling her pen between her fingers. "Okay, and what DNA have you gathered, Inspector?"

"Miss Holten, thank you for taking part, and you pose a very interesting question," he said, relaxing into his chair again.

She pouted but held his gaze.

"We're confident that Mr. Sparks and the victim, Mr. Dexter, had some sort of scuffle moments before the murder took place. Both men landed punches on each other. Oh, I've already noticed the marks on your knuckles, Mr. Sparks, so please don't feel the need to cover them now. And that, I have to say, was your downfall. You see, when you battered Mr. Dexter, you left behind some of your own blood. Thanks to the naughty little soliciting charge you received a few years ago, your DNA was already in our system. That alone is enough to get you to court."

"We will be applying for bail, Inspector," Miss Holten said. A red blush rose from the neck of her pristine white shirt.

Hamilton shrugged. "That kind of information is for the court. I'm here to make sure murderers are arrested and justice is served, for the victims and their families."

He turned his attention back to Michael. Infuriated with the man's lack of response, he was determined to entice a reaction. "I think we're finished for now. But just so you are aware, another interview will be conducted in due course regarding the other victims." Hamilton threw the bait as he gathered his notes together.

"Other victims?" Michael shouted, his resolve broken.

The man's solicitor shot him a warning look and shook her head.

Hamilton's excitement bubbled inside. *That was easier than I thought.* He gazed at Michael. "Yes, Mr. Sparks, the other victims. There have been six murder victims in our investigation. Mr. Dexter was just one of them."

The solicitor touched her client's shoulder. "So you've found my client's DNA at all the crime scenes, have you, Inspector?"

"No, Miss Holten, but our pathology team believe the same murder weapon was used on all six victims," Hamilton lied to coax the suspect further. "So you'll understand why we need to establish Mr. Sparks's whereabouts when the other murders took place."

"You're having a fucking laugh if you think you're pinning this on me." Michael's face contorted in anger.

"Mr. Sparks, I urge you to say nothing further in this interview," Miss Holten said.

"Shut up! What use are you to me? You're happy to just sit there and listen while they accuse me of murdering all those women. No, I won't have it."

"But you haven't denied murdering Mr. Dexter," Hamilton snapped eagerly.

"Very good, Inspector. I can see what you're trying to do here. I will not be a fool to your games. I am an innocent man." Michael's tone had calmed significantly.

"Mr. Sparks, we know that is not true. Your DNA was found on the victim—you will go to prison for his murder. And believe me when I tell you I will do everything in my power between now and the court hearing to connect you to all of the victims and prove you murdered them. You will never step foot in your precious theatre again." Hamilton's tone was low and deep, and he leaned forward on the table, his face inches from Michael's.

"Inspector, I request a break in this interview to consult with my client further," Miss Holten interrupted.

Hamilton nodded at Clarke, who stated the time before he stopped the recording.

"Advise your client wisely, Miss Holten. We'll be back shortly." Hamilton bundled his papers together and left the interview room.

CHAPTER FORTY-ONE

Grace staggered along the street to her home, occasionally holding on to a fence to steady herself. The sky was a sheet of blackness with the odd twinkling star, and she was relieved for the streetlights that illuminated her path. The air was bitter cold, but her coat, draped over her handbag, dragged on the ground beside her. She was vacant and uninterested in the disapproving glances from passers-by.

Rubbish from the small brown recycling bin had blown into the middle of Grace's front garden, and she tripped, grazing her hands on the ground. Lying face down on the wet grass, she almost laughed at herself and the state she was in. A whistle echoed through the trees, forcing her to turn over and sit up. She held her breath and peered around the quiet neighbourhood, back down the street she had just walked. *Nothing.* She exhaled, but the thump in her chest quickened as she fumbled in her handbag for her keys, never taking her eyes from the road. Once she had them tight in her grasp, she awkwardly lifted herself from the ground and stumbled to the front door, leaving her coat where it had fallen.

With the door shut behind her, Grace shook her head and laughed at herself. *For fuck's sake, pull yourself together.* But the crushing pain erupting in her skull made things difficult. Motown tunes blared from behind the kitchen door, Valerie's harmonies keeping up with each lyric. Although she tripped up the stairs twice, Lionel Richie covered her drunken blunders.

She sat motionless on the edge of her bed for half an hour, her mind incoherent. The alcohol sped through her system, the bedroom spun, and she desperately tried to ignore the queasiness simmering in her stomach. In an attempt to keep her mind from the sickly feeling, she finally shed the depressing funeral clothes and pulled on a baggy T-shirt and leggings. Without thinking, she retrieved the diary and pen from under her pillow, opened to a blank page, and started scribbling.

I don't even know what day it is any more… can it really still be the same day that Eric was cremated? The same day that his murderer was arrested? Wait! Not just any 'murderer' either. Michael!!! My boss. Eric's boss!! This shit can't be real. Ha ha, ha ha, ha ha!! I'm so stupid… I thought my bad dreams meant something. That I could help. Help who? Her or him? I can't even help myself. A psychic!! I couldn't even "see" that the man I loved was sleeping around or that he was murdered by someone I trusted. Someone I saw every day and thought of as a friend. But someone is watching me. I know it. During the night, when the streets are dark and quiet. What if it's the ghosts of the people I knew? What if they're watching me from the shadows??? OMG what is wrong with me? Paranoia central!!!! Grace, no one is watching you!!!!! Why would they? I'm useless. A pathetic waste of space who doesn't deserve the life I've been given.

She closed the book and flopped back onto the bed, allowing sleep to take her.

CHAPTER FORTY-TWO

Hamilton returned to the interview room with a confident attitude. The tension had eased away, and the knots in his shoulders had relaxed. He knew the solicitor had called for a break in the interview to encourage her client to make a full confession, and the miserable look on Michael's face confirmed that. He wanted the suspect's admission on tape so he could get home to his wife and give her the attention she deserved.

"Miss Holten tells me you're ready to cooperate with us now, Mr. Sparks," Hamilton said once Clarke had recorded the necessary details.

Michael lifted his head to meet Hamilton's glare. "On the condition that you understand I will not be stitched up for crimes I did not commit, Inspector."

"You're not in any position to stipulate conditions or strike up deals at the moment, Mr. Sparks. We're waiting to hear what you have to say."

An uncomfortable silence filled the room once again, and Hamilton worried the man was considering retaking the 'no comment' route. He needed to bide his time—he didn't want to put too much pressure on Michael. He narrowed his eyes, glaring directly at his suspect. Michael only lasted a few moments before peering down at the table. When he finally lifted his head, his face was ghastly pale.

"Tell them exactly what you told me," Miss Holten said.

"Okay… I admit that I killed Eric Dexter, but it was an accident, and I had nothing to do with the deaths of any of those women."

Hamilton and Clarke exchanged glances. He understood the look of disappointment in his partner's eyes.

"Continue, Mr. Sparks. We need to know everything, all the details from the night of Mr. Dexter's death." Hamilton could hear the downhearted tone in his own voice.

"I'll be honest with you, Inspector. Although I didn't particularly like the man, credit where it's due, he was a superb actor, and a lot of fans followed him to my theatre. However, I overheard Eric and Grace having a small altercation on opening night. From what they said, it was obvious they had slept together. While Emily was still alive, I might add. Disgusting behaviour, if you ask me."

"We have all of this information, Mr. Sparks."

Michael screwed up his face but continued as if he hadn't been interrupted. "Well, it was blatantly clear he had just used Grace to pass the time. That man cared about no one but himself. And the way he spoke to her that evening… it was appalling. Grace is a beautiful and exceptional woman, and I was infuriated when I heard him."

"So you murdered the man because you were jealous?" Clarke interjected.

Hamilton could sense the anger emanating from his partner, but he saw no need for aggression while the suspect was speaking freely.

"It wasn't murder! I've told you already, it was an unfortunate accident. And I was not jealous of that man—ha! But did I like the way he behaved or the way he spoke to my colleague? No, I bloody well did not."

"Unfortunate accident? You killed a man! And the way you're talking about Miss Murphy implies to me that you thought more of her than just a colleague," Clarke shot back.

Michael threw his hands up in the air and sighed. "Fine, I'll say no more."

Hamilton had dreaded that reaction and was infuriated that the confession had ceased mid-flow. Michael folded his arms across his chest and stared at the wall to his left. Clarke looked vexed and Hamilton shoved his knee against Clarke's thigh in warning. His partner grunted submission.

"Mr. Sparks, this is your chance to tell your side of the story. We already have your murder confession on tape, and that's enough for us. So, if you don't want to say any more, then we'll have you taken back to your cell."

Michael slowly turned to face the detectives again. Hatred oozed from his cold blue eyes, and his upper lip curved as though he were preparing to growl. "Yes, I'll have my say, Inspector." His face relaxed, and he inhaled dramatically through his nose.

Hamilton was surprised by his sudden change in character.

"Well, now you're ready to listen. During opening week, the crew and I visited a local bar for a few drinks after the performance. As I had driven in to work that day, I only had a few virgin martinis, of course. True to style, Eric enjoyed the attention and all the cocktails and shots people bought him. He missed the last train, so I offered to give him a lift home. I think he sobered up during the journey, or perhaps he had been putting on a show in the bar. I don't know, but I wanted to make sure he got home all the same—I'm not a monster. Anyway, once we were inside his apartment, he took a beer from the fridge and insisted that I stay for one. But then that foul mouth reared its ugly head again. He bragged about all the women he had slept with, taunted me for living with my mother, and called me hurtful names." Michael paused and looked down at his trembling hands resting on the table.

Hamilton silently urged the man to continue.

"You know, it's true when people say they see red. I never really believed it before. But that night, the red mist descended, and I punched him in the face," Michael lifted his head and glared directly at Hamilton. "I've never punched anyone before; it was liberating. But the size of Eric compared to me—I didn't think it had done much damage, especially when he charged at me. By the grace of God, my face was spared, but he did get a few jabs into my ribs. He pinned me up against the kitchen table, and I feared for my life. The glass fruit bowl was in reach, so I grabbed it and whacked it over his head. I just wanted to get free from his hold. It didn't smash but he slumped down in a heap. The blood poured from his head… I told you it was an accident."

"What about the knife you struck into his heart, Mr. Sparks?" Hamilton questioned.

"I panicked. I couldn't be sent to prison, with all those grimy delinquents, because of a stupid mishap. I had read all the details about the other murders, that the women had been stabbed through the heart. I thought if I stuck the knife into his chest, you'd assume it was the same killer and I'd be free. But I am not responsible for the women that were killed."

"Well, for Eric Dexter's sake, thank heavens for the DNA database, eh?" Clarke huffed, checked the time, and terminated the recording.

Hamilton turned to the uniformed policeman standing guard at the door. "Take this man down to the cell, officer."

"That's it? What happens now? What about a deal for my cooperation?" Michael fired questions at them, a look of terror cast over his face.

"We didn't promise any deal. Did we say anything about a deal, Sergeant?"

Clarke turned down his lips and shook his head in reply to Hamilton's question.

"You can't do this to me. I have rights. I told you the truth—I didn't murder those women." Michael continued to shout as the officer escorted him from the room, and Miss Holten silently followed them.

"Mr. Dexter had rights too, and you've just confessed to his murder. Your solicitor can explain the logistics of what will happen now," Hamilton countered as he walked away with his partner towards the front desk.

"Gov, I don't think I've ever felt so disappointed during a murder confession."

Hamilton sighed heavily. "I hear you, Lewis! Something awful tells me we're back to square one with this investigation."

****

The team listened intently while Clarke informed them of the results of Michael's interview and relayed the fear that it bore no significance on the other murders.

"That must have been bittersweet, Lewis. Kudos on getting the confession for Dexter's murder, but it pretty much leaves us up shit creek again with this case," said Wedlock, the first to make his opinion heard.

"Don't I know it?" Clarke pulled his hands through his jet-black hair in frustration. He was still vexed by Michael's blasé attitude about murdering a young man, accident or not.

"Maybe this doesn't lead us directly back to square one," Morris said. "What if Eric Dexter actually was our killer all along? I mean, we were about to arrest him before he was murdered, and there's been no female victims since his demise. What's not to say we were right?"

Clarke contemplated his colleagues' observation. "You could have something there, Sharon. But I can't help but wonder, did we really have enough evidence to make that stick? Despite what the boss thought, his hand was forced by the DCI to make that arrest."

"But that's exactly it—the boss *did* have doubts about Dexter, his gut was telling him there was something dubious about him," she continued to challenge him.

Spurred on by the debate, Fraser chimed in. "We can't make arrests on the boss's gut feeling, but you do have to admit that Dexter knew most of the victims. He was a prolific ladies' man."

"Christ! Being a ladies' man doesn't automatically make you a murderer, Kerry. And you have to remember there's been no sexual assault aspect to these crimes. I can't see it being Dexter's MO." Clarke found himself jumping to Eric's defence, mainly because their flirtatious personalities were starkly similar.

"Sounds like we've got a good debate going on in here." Hamilton startled the team, and Clarke wondered how much he had overheard.

"It's brilliant. I'm proud with how we're working as a team on this. We won't always agree, but if someone's theory leads us to a piece of evidence, a suspect, or even an arrest, then I'm happy to trash out suggestions all night."

Clarke prayed silently that his partner didn't actually mean *that* night. "What did the chief have to say?"

"He's already left for the day, so Betty booked me in to see him first thing."

The pause made Clarke groan—he knew exactly what was coming next.

"I know you're eager to get home, but I'm encouraged by what I've just heard from you all. If we crack on for another hour or so, I'm sure it'll help with my morning meeting. The last thing we want is for DCI Allen to file this investigation in the unsolved cases. Think of those women and their families," Hamilton said.

Clarke rolled his eyes at his partner's blatant endeavour to pull on their heartstrings. It had worked, though; he would never abandon Hamilton, so he jumped on the wagon to rally the team.

"The boss is right—we have to remember today was a victory. We've caught a killer. Granted, he wasn't exactly the one we wanted, but we shouldn't let that dishearten us. Let's use it to spur us on and find this son of a bitch."

Hamilton winked in his direction, and Clarke was glad that their combined effort had the desired effect. Within minutes, the team turned to their computers, the whiteboard and their case files, trying to unearth any vital clues they had missed.

CHAPTER FORTY-THREE

Valerie worried for her daughter. She watched her sleeping, curled up like a small child on a king-size bed, and wondered if Grace could be saved from the self-destructive road she was walking. She was pained to discover Grace had found comfort, yet again, at the bottom of a bottle rather than turning to her.

Her daughter's body was thinner than it had ever been, and her naturally rosy cheeks were sunken and pale. Valerie couldn't remember the last time they had shared a meal together. She felt like crying, but she knew once those floodgates opened they might never close again. The sight of her vulnerable offspring motivated her to be the strong one, but she was desperate for someone to help her.

She hoped exposing Grace's feeble state wouldn't be seen as an act of betrayal, but she couldn't ignore the downward spiral any longer. She crept out of the bedroom and down to the living room. She picked up her mobile phone and thumbed through the contacts, stopping at Natasha's name. Sometimes help could only come from a close friend, someone who didn't judge, patronise, and create useless arguments. Natasha was a go-getter, her positivity shone through her attitude, and Valerie knew only this friend could deliver the kick up the arse her daughter needed. She was deflated when the call went to voicemail, but comforted to hear Natasha's voice and not the standard automated one. Valerie left an urgent message.

A banging noise from upstairs startled her, but she bounced up the stairs instantly. She paused briefly outside Grace's bedroom to catch her breath. Facing her daughter head-on had never worked—Grace was stubborn and defensive, and would raise her guard the moment she thought anyone was instructing her how to behave. Valerie needed to be calm, so she gently knocked on the bedroom door, then again, a bit louder. Nothing. The loud racket from inside the room had stopped, and she could hear the faint sound of whimpering.

"Grace, can I come in?" Valerie asked as she turned the handle.

It moved in her hand, but the door remained closed. She continued to twist the doorknob, using her other hand to knock on the door. Her agitation grew.

"Why have you locked the door? Are you okay? You better not be drinking in there, Grace Murphy." She cringed at her utter lack of patience, but her temper grew the more she was ignored. "I'm telling you now, young lady, if you don't open this door, I'll find a way into that room. Do you hear me?"

"I just want to be on my own, Mum. Please go away!" Grace screamed.

"Don't push me away. I want to help you. Don't barricade yourself in. I won't even mention last night or the drinking."

"You just did!"

"Are you drinking now?"

"No!" Grace yelled again.

She closed her eyes and sighed. "I just want to help you."

"Well, I don't need your help."

"It's very frustrating talking to a piece of wood, Grace. Can you please just open it?"

"I don't want to see you, Mum. I can't bear to see the disappointment in your eyes, and I don't want a lecture about drinking, or my state of mind, or blah, blah, blah."

Valerie was exhausted and angry in equal measures. She couldn't argue with Grace. She was disappointed and saddened by her daughter's choices, but also furious with the lack of respect she was shown. She slid down to the floor, pulled her knees up, and let her head rest on the wall. No one spoke for half an hour.

"Don't you have an appointment with your psychiatrist today?" Valerie broke the silence. "Why don't you have a refreshing shower, something to eat, and I'll drive you there."

"I missed it. Overslept."

"Shall I call her and explain for you?"

"No."

"For crying out loud, Grace!" Valerie jumped up and yelled towards the door. "Pull yourself together and stop wallowing in self-pity. When are you going to realise you're not the only person grieving? I know you're having a rough time of it, but I'm trying to help. Stop feeling sorry for yourself."

"I'm not asking for your help," Grace whispered.

Valerie slumped her shoulders. She could hear the change in her daughter's tone; the façade had been dropped. "It's okay to accept support."

She was ignored again, but was confident this time it was because of sadness, not rage. Had she pushed Grace too far? Should she have stayed away? Would it be best to leave and let her daughter make her own mistakes? The questions mounted, and she scraped her fingers through her hair, feeling confused. Grace sobbed, sounding clearer and closer than before. In that moment, all of Valerie's questions were answered. She sank to the floor again, sat cross-legged, and stared at the door—beyond it, her daughter was breaking down. She just waited. She would wait until Grace was ready to let her in.

CHAPTER FORTY-FOUR

Hamilton cleared his throat to grab Betty's attention. "Oh! Denis, I'm sorry I didn't hear you come in." She'd been working between the computer and a pile of handwritten notes.

"It's only eight a.m. but you look like you've been at it for hours already."

"Well my boss is DCI Allen. I don't have time to sit here filing my nails." She laughed at her own joke.

Hamilton chuckled. He couldn't help but like the woman. Though he was unsure of her age, he guessed she was easily a decade older than he was, maybe two. So she could have been anywhere from forty-five upwards; he was useless at guessing women's ages. Grey strands ran through her hair, threatening to overtake the once-jet-black locks, but she hadn't succumbed to the vanity of covering them up with dye. She always smelt of musk, a scent his mother had loved dearly.

"You can go straight in, Denis. He's waiting for you," she said with a smile then hurried back to her paperwork.

"Thanks, Betty." He returned her smile and walked through the grand oak door.

Hamilton hoped his face wouldn't betray the nervousness he felt inside. He was content with his team and the effort they had made, but he was worried Allen would not extend the same encouragement.

"Morning, Denis. Take a seat and give me an update."

Hamilton noted the unfriendly tone in his boss's voice. He sat in the chair opposite Allen and recounted the interview with Michael Sparks, as well as the determination and hard work his team had demonstrated before leaving the station the previous evening. He was pleased the DCI listened without interrupting.

"It seems you and your team have a catch-22 situation, Denis. If the murderer doesn't strike again, you're at a loss. And if he does, it sounds like you would need him to slip up considerably and leave DNA, which seems out of character for him." The DCI frowned and rubbed his temples with his index fingers— that was never a positive sign. "I think you can guess where I'm inclined to go with this investigation. It's not like other cases aren't piling up."

"Chief, you've heard the effort everyone put in after Sparks's interview. It hasn't deterred them from wanting to catch this lunatic. We owe it to the victims' families to give it one last try. The team have worked hard on this plan, and it may just lead to some viable leads. Let us see it through," Hamilton said with a desperation in his tone.

"My superiors won't like this one little bit, Denis. The exposure in the media has died down, and that's the way my boss wants to keep it. There's already been an outcry about the Met's lack of suspects and convictions with this one."

Allen swiveled his chair round and glared out the window for a few moments. Hamilton said nothing but was eager to know what his boss was thinking.

As though Allen read his mind, he turned back with a grave expression. "Denis, let me share something with you. Many years ago, I was involved in a case where two young boys, just ten years old, went missing. There was no evidence, and the leads were slim. Some people were adamant they had been kidnapped, while others said they had just upped and run away. We never found them. The file slipped into the unsolved cases, and I've hated myself ever since that day for not bringing justice, or peace of mind, to their families. Their little faces still haunt me."

Hamilton was taken by surprise; his DCI had never divulged anything personal to him in the three years they had worked together. He was contemplating a reply, but Allen continued speaking.

"Therefore, I'm inclined to agree with you. If this is the one last push we can give to the case, then you have my backing. Not only for the families involved but also for you and your team, so you can all sleep at night with the knowledge that you did everything in your power."

"Thank you, chief."

"Now get out of here so I can deliver the news to my boss. It's not going to be a pleasant phone conversation, I can assure you."

Although the parting words were stern, the twinkle in Allen's eye forced Hamilton to view the man in a new light. Gratified to know his superior would cover his back, he left the office with a spring in his step.

He bounced through the incident room door with hopes that his newfound determination would prove infectious to his team. He gathered them together and detailed his discussion with Allen, omitting the chief's shared memory, which would, for now at least, stay between just the two of them.

"This is our last chance to stir up the public and get every single shred of information we can. We need their help—it's the only way we're going to get a breakthrough in the case. Thanks to the detailed plan we devised last night, we all know what we should be doing. So let's get on with it," Hamilton ordered enthusiastically.

"Sir, a quick word please." Fraser approached him once their colleagues were occupied with their tasks. "I thought about all the ideas we came up with last night in order to gain the public's help. If I'm honest, I'm furious with myself for not thinking of this before. With your permission, I would like to create a Facebook page."

"Tell me more, Kerry."

"Sorry, sir, I'm not being very clear. What I mean is, if I have a Facebook page in place before our *Crimewatch* appeal, we can advertise it on the show. That way, the public can interact with us via Facebook. Not only is there a public wall for people who are happy to share their thoughts, but there's also the option of private messages. Only we could access these, and we can highlight that level of security on the show."

"Sometimes the beauty of a phone call is its complete anonymity, Kerry, but I do like your thinking, and I'm not going to rule out any form of communication with the public."

"We can also use it to share the victims' photographs and our contact details. Once the show has aired, we can have a recording of it playing from the Facebook page for anyone that may have missed it." Fraser spoke with such passion and excitement about the social media angle of the case, Hamilton couldn't dampen her spirit.

"Kerry, I love it! Create the page and then liaise with Sharon once she's got the go-ahead from *Crimewatch*," he said, before Morris called him over.

"What is it, Sharon?"

"Brilliant news, boss! I've just ended the call to my contact at the BBC Studios, and she's confident that with a high-profile case like ours, and the fact that we're looking for a serial killer, the bosses at *Crimewatch* will give us a special episode. They'll do short reconstructions for all five women, detailing their last movements."

"That's fantastic, Sharon! Really positive leaps we're taking. Let's just hope there's someone out there who has the information we need." Hamilton watched Fraser busy at the computer while Clarke and Wedlock released an appeal for all the national newspapers.

"Sharon, once you've got all the details in place, I want you to work with Kerry. She's thought of another avenue we can explore to grab the public's attention." She nodded in response and returned to the phone.

A tingle of excitement soared through Hamilton's body. *We're coming for you, you piece of scum.*

CHAPTER FORTY-FIVE

The television remained silent and blank, acting as just a source of Grace's reflection as she stared at the unused device. Newspapers were discarded in the bin, and she'd deleted any news-affiliated apps from her phone. She feared she would be forced to hear news about Michael, his arrest, and the deaths of her friends all over again.

Disappointed with herself, Grace thought isolation was best if she wanted to avoid alcohol and lectures. She hadn't contacted Maria since missing her appointment a week ago, but uncertainty niggled in the back of her mind. She'd been excited about the plans she had made with her psychiatrist. Had things really changed so drastically to make her not want to leave the safety of her bedroom?

The abandoned diary came to mind, and she reached under the pillow for it. She frowned—it wasn't there. She glanced around her room and realised she couldn't remember the last time she had used it, let alone seen it. On a whim, she opened the drawer of the bedside table. The diary rested there, calling to her like a beacon. *Why would I have put it in there? When did I put it in there?* She screwed up her face, confused, and pulled it out of the drawer, eager to read the last entry.

Grace thumbed to a page with scribbled words all over it. She hardly recognised her own handwriting. The barely legible date at the top informed her it had been written the day of Eric's funeral. *That was the last time I had a drink. I have absolutely no memory of writing this.* She read over her own words and felt as if she were snooping through a stranger's diary. Her eyes hung on the word *pathetic,* and she felt hurt and saddened by the self-image.

Something in her peripheral vision caught her eye, and she looked up from the journal. The white feather she'd found at the cemetery had drifted from her computer table to the floor, although the window was closed and there was no breeze in the room. She stood up and crossed the room. Bending down onto one knee, she picked it up and clutched it in her hand, holding it over her heart. *I miss you, granddad.*

Her thoughts filled with images of the man she had placed on a pedestal. She saw him clearly in her mind, wearing his favourite sky-blue wooly jumper and a pair of grey suit trousers. Grace had always laughed at her grandfather's stubborn commitment to wearing only suit trousers. It had taken her years to get him out of his formal patent-black shoes, but when she'd found a pair of plain black Velcro trainers, he'd reluctantly agreed they were a suitable alternative. But he refused point blank to wear anything but his trousers, which he had in every colour, and could never fathom the obsession with jeans.

Although the memory brought with it some sadness, it also infused her with a feeling of strength and an uncontrollable desire to get out of the house. *I am not pathetic. Or useless! I will not let myself sink into despair, continually reaching for the bottle.* A fire ignited in Grace's stomach, and she rushed into the shower to wash away the hopeless feeling that had been dragging her down. Once dried and dressed, she left the confines of her bedroom— something she hadn't done in days.

She was pleased to find the house empty; Valerie had already left for work. Grace left a note to explain she needed some fresh air and wouldn't be long, so as not to worry her mother. Ignoring the sensible thought of wrapping up warmly, Grace welcomed the crisp breeze on her face once she was outside. As she walked along the streets, with no particular destination in mind, she felt free.

After wandering around in a daze for over an hour, she was surprised to find herself outside Maria's address. Her finger hesitated over the bell. She thought how rude it was of her to turn up unannounced, particularly after missing their last session.

Well, you're here now—just go for it. She pressed the white button and waited anxiously.

"Grace! Well, now there's a face I wasn't expecting." Maria answered the door in her usual jolly manner, that genuine warmth still present in her voice.

Overwhelmed by the friendly greeting, Grace stunned herself as tears erupted down her cheeks. She attempted an apology, and an explanation of some kind, but her words were jumbled through the unexpected emotional outpour.

"Oh, my dear! What's all this?" Maria asked as she stepped outside her front door and placed an arm around Grace's shoulder. "Come inside. You're freezing. There's nothing that a decent cup of tea can't help fix."

She snorted a half-laugh, half-cry sound at Maria's typical Irish suggestion that tea was the remedy to everything. There was comfort wrapped in Maria's embrace.

"We'll have this drink downstairs. This isn't a session, so I'll happily open my home to you."

Maria led Grace into a cosy sitting room with a roaring log fire on one side. It was filled with bookcases, antiques, and flowery decor. The burgundy three-piece suite was old—frayed material gave away its years of wear—but it was clean and inviting. Grace suddenly realised her legs ached from the long walk, and she gladly sank into the large armchair.

Maria handed her a box of tissues. "Wipe the tears, dear. I'll give you a minute to yourself while I brew the tea."

Grace appreciated the kind woman's gesture and used the time alone to dry her face. Pushing the sadness deep down, she recalled the determination she'd found earlier.

"Looks like the fire has warmed you up nicely. There's a nice glow in your cheeks now." Maria settled two mugs of tea on the table between them. "I can't believe you were out in this weather without a coat on."

"I didn't feel how cold it was. I guess I didn't really feel much of anything," she confessed, staring into the flames. "It wasn't my plan to come here. Actually, there was no plan. I just needed to get out of the house."

She decided it was time to fully open up to Maria, and she spent the next half an hour detailing the harrowing events she had faced since Christmas, including a subject she hadn't approached with her psychiatrist: her grandfather.

"It's the first real grief and loss that has affected me. Mostly, I'm okay and can get on with everyday life, feel normal. Then there are other days when I can hardly breathe with the pain. Something as little as a photo or a song can set me off, and that'll be it. It crushes me that I can't see him."

"Grace, you're not only dealing with the anguish of losing a close relative, but there's the death of your friends and colleagues also. It gives me a picture as to why you're suffering such horrifying nightmares."

Maria paused and sighed heavily.

"What is it?" Grace asked

"Are you still serious about working with me to uncover your dreams? I have to say, I think we've made progress here today. You have finally dropped your defensive walls and let me in, about your past and your present emotional pain. I thank you for that, Grace. There are factors in your life that are deeply troubling, and I believe you could benefit from hypnosis therapy."

"I'll try anything that can rid me of these bad dreams and hopefully the misery I'm falling into. I want peace. Gosh, I want to sleep! I feel comfortable with you, Maria, and I trust you. So yes, I'm willing to explore it with you."

Maria beamed. "I'm glad, Grace. I want to help you. I'd like to spend some intense time with you. I can fully explain what the hypnosis state is to you, so you're fully informed about what we'll do and how it works. It will give you a chance to ask me any questions and make sure you feel at ease before we start. Let me try and clear my diary for a week's time so we can spend a few days together. That way, we won't have to put a restricted time limit on ourselves in one session a week. I think one more cuppa is in order before you leave. Maybe your mum could collect you?"

Maria returned to the kitchen while Grace sent a text message and received a speedy reply. While the pair waited for Valerie to arrive, they talked openly with one another. She enquired about Maria's family and discovered the woman had one sister and a niece, both of whom lived in Northern Ireland, and rarely spoke to her.

"I'll let you into a little secret—I'm actually going to take a step back from full-time work shortly. Of course I'll have a few select clients, like yourself, but I plan to free up at least three days a week to write a book." She raised her eyebrows and pulled a funny face before launching into a passionate speech about her creative ideas.

By the time Grace left Maria's home, she was eager to begin her hypnosis therapy, and also felt she had made a dear friend in her psychiatrist.

****

Grace contemplated diverting the call to voicemail again, but she also felt guilty about ignoring Natasha. The silent iPhone buzzed on her computer table, a picture of the two friends clinking champagne glasses filled the screen, and the green and red options demanded she make a choice.

"Hello."

"Finally! Where the fuck have you been? I've been calling you for days, woman," Natasha cried down the phone in her usual ballsy tone.

"I've had a lot to deal with."

"You're telling me! That's what I've been trying to contact you about."

"I guess you've seen it all in the papers." Grace sighed.

"Who needs newspapers when you're the attending solicitor?"

"What the hell are you talking about?"

"Erm… I'm talking about yours truly being called for by the police station to represent one Mr. Michael Sparks on a murder charge."

"No way—I don't believe you! But you know him personally. Is that even allowed?"

"Okay, firstly, I don't know him, *know him*. I'm just aware he's your boss. And secondly, if the money is right, I can represent whoever I want to. Anyway, he isn't my client. Mr. Forde was on a business trip, and it was an urgent call, so I took it. He'll represent him during the court case."

"So there will be a court case?"

"Of course! Grace, the man admitted to murder."

She was silent. It was one thing to witness his arrest, but it was a complete shock to hear that he had actually confessed.

"The thing is…" Natasha dragged out her sentence. "It's only Eric he killed."

"I don't understand. I thought all the murders were connected." Grace frowned.

Natasha explained what had been disclosed during Michael's interview after he was arrested. *Shit! So the murderer is still out there. Can that be possible?* A swirling sensation erupted in her stomach, along with a feeling of unease. She barely noticed Natasha had continued chattering.

"Honestly, I'm sure Mr. Forde's son could have handled the interview, but I thought I might spot some talent. Let me tell you, that clearly does not exist in the Metropolitan Police Service. If I want a man in uniform, I think I'll stick to the fire brigade. Or maybe just keep a dress-up box in my bedroom for visitors."

"Seriously, Tash, is that all you think about?" Grace's impatience to end the call grew as her friend's mind had obviously drifted elsewhere.

"Better believe it, chick. I'm all about getting the man, so stay out of my way when I'm on the prowl." Natasha mocked an evil laugh.

"Thanks for the chat, and the info, but I really have to go. I'll call you soon. Bye."

She hung up the phone before Natasha had the chance to protest. She sank onto the chair and drummed her fingers repeatedly on the computer desk. Her eyes darted from side to side, scanning her mind and devising a plan. *Maybe I can still help catch the killer.*

CHAPTER FORTY-SIX

Once they were in the office, Maria took a moment to study Grace and was pleased to find she appeared less emotional than she had during their last encounter.

"Make yourself comfortable. I'll put the kettle on." She quickly prepared the essential cups of tea and rejoined the young girl. She was eager to begin and move Grace forward with her therapy. "I apologise for the break in our sessions. It took me longer than expected to clear my diary, but you have my undivided attention now. I'm completely free this week, and we can work together as much as you're happy to. I'm even contemplating a little holiday in the sun for myself the following week."

"Perks of being self-employed." Grace relaxed, lying back on the reclining chair, and Maria smiled.

"Have you thought any more about using this therapy technique to uncover your nightmares?"

"I feel more determined than ever. I've recently found out that my boss did not murder all those women, and I can't help but wonder if I'm supposed to help them. My mum thinks it's all nonsense, and it may well be, but I have to know for sure."

"Firstly, you need to know that some people are very susceptible to hypnosis. Others, not so much. This is completely down to the individual and has a lot to do with how much they trust their psychiatrist."

"I trust you completely, Maria."

She felt reassured by Grace's quick reply. "I'm glad to hear that, dear. I have a personal belief that many people don't understand the hypnotic state or even appreciate it, for that matter. It's the point right before sleep, where you're so comfortable you don't want to move. You can, of course, but you're just so relaxed, you won't want to." She paused to ensure Grace was happy with the information so far before she continued.

"Because we're using this kind of therapy to uncover your dreams, an area that creates a crisis in your life, we'll set up a safe harbour for you before I induce this hypnotic state. Have a think about what you want your safe place to be—perhaps somewhere you've been before or somewhere you've seen in a photograph. But it should be a place that you feel safe, calm, and peaceful, so it needs to be a strong image for you. Use all your senses: the colours you see, the sounds you hear or perhaps the silence, the smells of that place and what your skin can feel. Perhaps you're walking through damp grass or lying on soft sand."

"I have somewhere in mind. My granddad's resting place. I always feel close to him there. But why do I need this safe place? I'm in no danger while I'm in this state, am I?" Grace asked.

"There's no need to worry. As I've said, the visions you suffer are traumatic for you. Therefore, if I think you're becoming agitated during the hypnosis, I can guide you to your safe place to help you calm down."

"What happens if I want to come out of it? Can I do that on my own?"

"Of course. There are certain commands we can use. So in the case of waking yourself up, I will say, 'Anytime you find yourself uncomfortable and want to return to full consciousness, all you need to do is cross your arms, and you'll be wide awake and back in the present.' If I feel that you're slipping too deep into the hypnotic state, and I want to bring you back to a comfortable level, I'll use your name, 'Grace, move your left arm slightly,' or 'Grace, are you comfortable?'" She paused. "How does that make you feel? Are you still happy to go ahead with the therapy?"

Maria wanted to giggle when Grace removed a pad and pen from her handbag, but she suppressed the urge and remained professional.

"I'm worried I won't remember all of this. Can you repeat the commands so I can jot them down and memorise them?"

"Please don't fret. Before we begin, I'll repeat the commands so they're fresh in your mind. Don't put added stress on yourself by trying to memorise them. It will be more fluid and natural when we begin. I just wanted you to be aware of the basics. Are you okay with all of this?" Maria began to worry that she had overloaded the young patient too soon. She reached over the table and placed her hand on Grace's to comfort her. "We can stop any time you like."

"That's a relief, and I certainly have a much better understanding of the process now. I've read quite a lot about hypnotherapy on the Internet in the last few weeks, but it's different hearing it from you. You have made it sound much simpler. I just hope I remember all the commands correctly."

"Well, I'd like to do a preliminary session today. This is standard practice—a test, if you like—to find out how susceptible you are to the therapy."

Grace chewed her bottom lip but nodded. "What do I have to do?"

"Just lie as you are and relax."

Maria dimmed the lights and taped a black dot on the wall directly across from Grace, just above her eye level and the framed photographs. "Place your hands on either the chair or your lap, whichever is more comfortable for you."

She sat down again and altered her voice to a soft hum that worked well for her patients under hypnosis. "Grace, breathe deeply while you focus on the spot in front of you and listen to the sound of my voice. When I count one, you will close your eyes until I say two. When I do, you will open your eyes and focus your attention on the spot again. When I count three, you will close your eyes again until I say four. Continue to open and close your eyes as I count."

She paused to study her patient, whose eyes were firmly on the spot. *This might be easier than I thought.* "Your eyelids will begin to feel heavier and heavier as I count. You will feel so relaxed that you'll want to keep them closed and fall into a deep, peaceful state. Okay. One, close your eyes. Let all the muscles around your eyes relax. Breathe steadily and freely." Maria watched her table clock and waited sixty seconds.

"Two, open your eyes and focus on the spot. Let the relaxation flow from your eyes down to your cheeks." Grace's breathing relaxed as Maria continued to count.

She smiled as she knew they had reached the point she'd been waiting for. "Seven, close your eyes. Feel that relaxation now flowing from your eyelids down your cheeks, into your shoulders and neck. It is so relaxing that you don't want to open your eyes, and even if you tried, they would not open. Try to open your eyes."

Maria exhaled in relief as she watched her patient attempt to open her eyes. She had worried that maybe Grace wasn't a suitable candidate for hypnosis, given her vulnerable state, but the young girl just proved her receptiveness. *Perhaps too much so. I'll have to be careful not to let her go too deep.* Maria continued to count to ten, giving the commands to encourage relaxation. She then sipped her tea and gave Grace a few moments of tranquillity before she began the count up.

"In a moment, I'm going to count from one to five. When I reach the number five, you will open your eyes and feel wide awake."

Grace opened her eyes easily at the count of five and smiled. "That was so peaceful, a bit surreal, but I felt safe that I could follow your voice. How do you think I did?"

"Brilliantly, you were very open and responsive to the therapy. I'm glad you feel so positive. I do too."

Maria turned the lights back up and walked over to the alcove in the corner of the office. She flicked on the kettle and set about making a fresh cup of tea for Grace. She didn't do so after every session, but her fondness for the young lady continued to grow.

"Just one more cuppa to warm you up, make sure you don't feel too relaxed before you leave here." She giggled.

"Thank you. I'd appreciate that." Grace yawned.

"What I've scheduled is for you to come back the day after tomorrow, in the afternoon, and we'll truly begin the hypnosis in order to uncover those nightmares of yours."

Once Grace had left the office, Maria spent the rest of the afternoon making notes about the session. It had been a long time since she felt so excited about helping a patient.

CHAPTER FORTY-SEVEN

The incident room was uncharacteristically subdued when Hamilton returned from yet another meeting with DCI Allen. The gloominess could easily have been attributed to everyone being deep in thought about the impending outcome of the murder case. He noticed the newspaper on Clarke's desk.

"I can understand today's article has probably stirred some mixed reactions with us all," Hamilton said.

"Why do I feel so crappy about it?" Clarke slumped in his chair. "I should be over the moon that Sparks was refused bail."

Wedlock grunted. "Don't worry, Lewis. You're not alone. It's difficult. On the one hand, we got the guy, and he'll definitely serve time, but on the other, he wasn't the serial killer we were expecting to nail."

Hamilton exhaled deeply. "Look, I don't want to stand here and patronise you all with a false pep talk on how we can make this situation better."

"What did the chief say?" Morris interrupted.

He searched for the appropriate response. Backed into a corner, he hated being the bearer of bad news, but he knew he owed it to his team to be the one to tell them directly.

"We've been instructed to close the case and, for now at least, add it to the unsolved murder files. An alert will be placed on the system, which will immediately notify us of any similar crimes committed in the future. It doesn't mean it's over," he finally said.

He sensed their deflated mood, but none of them voiced an opinion. The dissatisfaction was clear, but he wondered if any of them felt like a failure as he did. He needed a reaction from them. "So come on, I want to know your feelings about this decision."

"It sucks, gov, but what can we do?" Wedlock called out. "There hasn't been a female victim for two months, and our media plea has dried up."

Morris agreed with her colleague. "Our *Crimewatch* appeal was four weeks ago, sir and frankly, we've been chasing our tails with those insignificant leads."

Hamilton nodded. He was fully aware of the details, but to hear his team speak them aloud gave him a clear indication of how they felt. He looked at Fraser, the sergeant he believed had contributed several brilliant ideas to the case. She was also the shyest member of the team, and he wanted to ensure her opinion was voiced before it was too late.

"Kerry, you're quiet. How do you feel about this decision?"

"It's difficult, sir. The verdict has been decided. It's out of our hands."

"What if it were in your hands? Would you have made the same call?"

Kerry's cheeks flushed red. "It's unfair to put me in that position, sir. But I suppose, in all honesty, yes, I would have felt I had to. These guys have already made valid points about the lack of evidence and clues. From my perspective, the social media side of things is like a ghost town. It's completely quiet online. When I post a status or retweet the victims' photos, there's barely a response any more." She looked down and fumbled with her fingers. "But there's another side of me that's carrying the burden of guilt for the victims and their families. I feel as though we've done them an injustice by not finding the killer. I almost don't want to admit to myself that the investigation is about to join the unsolved files."

Hamilton appreciated his team's candor, and Fraser's statement had echoed the one he'd spoken through with Allen. He was also anxious that the guilt would plague them all long after they had walked away from the case.

He assured them of the support they would be offered and urged them to approach him if they needed to talk to someone in the future. Morris and Wedlock glanced at each other and continued with their paperwork. As long-serving members of the Met, they had, unfortunately, already been involved with other unsolved cases. Fraser, however, remained quiet, and Hamilton made a mental note to check in with her. This wasn't an investigation he felt entirely comfortable abandoning, and he knew she felt the same.

CHAPTER FORTY-EIGHT

Maria opened the front door, feeling buoyant about her afternoon session and pleased to see her patient wearing the same excited expression. "Come in, Grace. Go on upstairs and make yourself comfortable."

Believing it better to begin the hypnosis straight away, Maria bypassed the tea-making routine. *We'll share a cuppa afterwards, while we discuss the session.* She watched Grace sink onto her usual spot on the reclining sofa. The young girl lifted her legs and curled them underneath her bottom, depicting a friendly vibe.

"I want to make sure you are completely comfortable in going forward with this therapy, because we will attempt to go deeper than our last session."

Grace nodded enthusiastically. "It's okay. You don't need to keep asking. I understand. I'm comfortable, and I'm willing."

She was encouraged by her patient's confident reply. "Fantastic. But we will take this at your pace. And if I feel you're going too deep into the hypnotic state, you'll hear me call your name, and you'll return to your safe place."

Maria carried out the same movements as before: she dimmed the lights and taped the black dot in exactly the same place. "I want you to remember, Grace, that anytime you want to return to full consciousness, just cross your arms over your chest, and you'll be back in the present. Most patients don't feel comfortable talking in their hypnotic state, and that's absolutely fine. So I want you to relax, rest your hands on your lap, and when I ask you a question, just signal yes by moving your left hand or no with your right hand."

Grace stretched out her legs and placed her hands where she had been instructed to. She inhaled deeply and exhaled slowly as she focused on the spot, and Maria was impressed with the young woman's commitment.

"We'll begin with the counting technique we used in our last session to help you relax, and then we'll begin to delve deeper."

Maria waited a few moments, allowing the silence to take over the room and for Grace to fall deeper into her hypnotic state. She observed her patient, a figure of serenity desperate to unmask her dreams. Using the same soft, whisper-like tone, Maria gave the counting commands and instructed Grace to open and close her eyes; to again focus on her breathing and the black dot until she was so relaxed she could no longer open her eyes.

"I want you to imagine your safe place. Picture it clearly in your mind. What kind of day is it? Is the sun shining down on you, or can you feel the rain wet against your skin? Think about what you can see and smell around you. Is the ground beneath you soft and inviting? Walk barefoot and feel it between your toes. Let your senses take over and entice a feeling of safety." Maria didn't expect answers to her questions—they were a technique to lead her patient into a sense of security.

"Grace, do you feel safe?"

This time Maria was answered with a twitch of Grace's left hand.

She smiled at the young girl's susceptible nature. She continued to observe Grace for a few more minutes before attempting to go deeper into her subconscious. Grace's breathing was steady and calm. A peaceful expression etched on her face.

"Grace, are you ready to go further into your thoughts?"

She moved the fingers on her left hand again.

"I want you to think about the nightmares you've suffered. Remember how they made you feel. Bring those dreams to the forefront of your mind. Go deeper into the memory of them. Visualise yourself in them as they are happening, actually watch them play out in your mind. Why do they entice a feeling of fear? Who or what can you see?"

Grace's chest rose and fell faster.

"Remember you can return to your safe place whenever you want. Do you want to return to your safe place, Grace?"

The right hand on her lap moved quickly, signalling a negative answer.

"Okay, remain relaxed. Slowly, take yourself to the scene you witnessed and relive it in your mind. What couldn't you see in your dream the first time that you can see now? How does it make you feel this time? Use all your senses once again. What can you see in your nightmares?"

Grace frowned and pinched her lips together as if she were in pain. Her body remained still, stiff almost, but the sound of her breathing took over the room as she inhaled and exhaled deeply through her nose.

Maria feared the visions were causing Grace serious discomfort. "Do you want to return to your safe place until you feel at ease again?"

There was no hand movement.

"Grace, are you comfortable?"

Maria waited, but her patient offered no communication. She wondered if she had allowed Grace to slip too far into a hypnotic state. "Grace, remember you can cross your arms and wake up anytime you want to. You can come back to the present, away from your visions."

There was a moment of calm as the young girl's breathing returned to a steady rhythm. She sighed relief as Grace's arms slowly lifted into the air. She crossed them over her chest and opened her eyes.

Maria was aware that some patients felt nervous and vulnerable when they first woke from their hypnotic state. She quietly leaned closer to the young woman and continued speaking in her soft voice. "Grace, how do you feel?"

Moments passed, and she speculated whether or not Grace had fully emerged from the hypnosis. As though their minds were in sync, Grace hurled her head to the side and glared in Maria's direction. She gasped. An ugly appearance, with eyes as dark as coal, had replaced the warm and peaceful expression she'd witnessed just moments before. Her fear increased as Grace cracked the knuckles on each of her fingers—an action Maria had never observed in any of their previous sessions. A chill trembled down her spine.

"Grace, are you okay?"

The young girl swung her legs round and planted them on the floor with a heavy thud. She slithered closer to the edge of her seat, her face inches from the psychiatrist's, a frown etched on her face. The breath from her flared nostrils wafted over Maria.

"Stop calling me that, for fuck's sake! My name is Carly."

CHAPTER FORTY-NINE

Carly crept slowly around the office, satisfied with her accomplishment. She sneered at Maria and felt more powerful every time the woman flinched.

"This is quite the dilemma for me. I can feel that Grace really admired you," Carly said, scratching the inside of her palm. "I just can't have you wandering around, knowing my secret."

"What makes you think I know anything?" Maria's lips quavered as she spoke.

Carly shrieked with laughter, making the psychiatrist recoil once again. "Because I know you're not an idiot. Are you an idiot, doc?"

"Who's asking, you or Grace?"

"Feisty. I like it. Shows you know who you're talking to, though, doesn't it?"

"I don't presume to know who you are, Carly, but yes, I can surmise what's going on here."

Carly flopped down on the reclining chair once again, but this time, it wasn't to get comfortable. She casually crossed her legs and arms, peering at her watch as she did. Her eyes darted to Maria, and she glared intently.

"There's still time on the clock, shrink, so analyse me. Why don't you tell me what's going on 'ere?"

Maria hesitated. "Well, multiple personalities—or 'dissociative identity disorder' as it's now known—is not my area of expertise, but I've read about the condition."

Carly laughed at Maria's attempt to sound confident and in control. In an instant, the cackle ceased, and she gestured with her hand for the psychiatrist to continue.

"I'll take that smirk on your face as affirmation." Maria gulped. "You have a mental disorder whereby at least two personalities control a person's behaviour. I'm assuming Grace is the host identity, as she's had the majority of control, and the memory loss, and she clearly knows nothing about her alternate personality. That would be you."

Carly slowly clapped her hands. The sound grew louder and louder as she rose from her seat. "You know quite a bit then, don't you, doc?"

"From what I understand, the disorder is an effect of severe trauma during early childhood. Grace could have been battling with this for some time. It's a coping mechanism for the patient, and the extra stress of losing her grandfather –"

"Don't you dare talk about him!" Carly pinched the psychiatrist's cheek with brute force. Maria swallowed hard, and the woman's fear thrilled her. "You have no right to mention him, you bitch." She pushed Maria's face to the side, leaving red fingerprints on her pale skin. "Grace is a weak, depressed fool who couldn't handle life after he died, and she turned to the bottle. Lucky for me, really, because it meant she didn't have the strength to suppress me. I was free from her." She walked to the table and perched on the edge, glad to see that Maria had made no attempt to move from her seat.

"And thanks to you, doc, I no longer have to be suppressed. I'm the stronger one. I can't be ignored any more." Carly slammed her fist against the table as her rage bubbled to the surface.

"So you know what the nightmares mean?" Maria whispered.

"Of course I know. They're not nightmares. They are memories trying to worm their way into her consciousness. Stupid cow thought she was clairvoyant or something." She sniggered and clawed at her palm again.

"Memories of what, Carly?"

"Doc! Well, well, well… shame on you. Grace gave you far too much credit. You're not the intelligent woman she regarded you as, if you haven't connected the dots." She grinned menacingly and winked, delighted to see the concentration on Maria's face, trying to piece everything together.

"You murdered those women."

"Bravo, Doctor Lee!" Carly clapped again.

"But why?"

She exhaled deeply, closed her eyes, and threw her head to the side dramatically. "Oh, you know, I have my reasons."

"The nightmares Grace suffered about the naked women and the blood, the reason she woke up feeling petrified, is because of you. She had distant memories of the crimes you committed when your personality had control."

"All right, woman! Calm down. It was a fucking joke when I said you could analyse me. I know how to deal with my grief. When people piss me off, double-cross me or my family, or generally act like a slag, they don't deserve to live. Not when other people are suffering, with no dignity left and die painfully through illnesses." She hopped up, sat fully on the table, and scratched her hand. "I targeted people who aren't worthy of the life they've been given, individuals who should be caring for the patients in their hospice, like my granddad. The scum of this world who use drink and drugs as an excuse for their stupidity, those that cheat and gloat."

"Grace has a drinking problem."

"I told you, weak and stupid. And she's gone forever too now. I've never felt as powerful as I do right now."

"Are you in some kind of partnership with Michael Sparks?"

"Ha! That leech? No, I am not. He lurked around all the time, peering at Grace. She was even more the sucker for never noticing how he felt about her. Everyone else bloody knew. I nearly lucked out with him, though, soppy fool. I can't believe he killed Eric in a jealous rage. I mean, I wasn't Eric's biggest fan, but I thought he'd finally show Grace some fun, and he encouraged the drinking, which was a good thing for me. Actually, Michael slightly impressed me, for once. But I can't believe he tried to fool the police with my calling card—the knife to the chest."

"Why is that your calling card, Carly?"

She jumped from the table and flew at Maria again. She stopped within inches of the psychiatrist's face. "Because I am sick and tired of letting other people break my heart. They abandon me or betray me or try to make me jealous. Well, no fucking more, they won't. I showed them who's in control." Spittle flew from Carly's mouth as she spoke. She returned to her seat on the table. "The problem is, what do we do now? You know too much."

"This is a counselling session; I sign a confidentiality contract to protect all my patients. I wouldn't go to the police about anything that we've uncovered today."

Ignoring her, Carly slipped off the table. She turned her back on Maria and mumbled to herself about what she should do. *The woman has a point. These sessions are all cloak-and-dagger. And I know Grace really liked this one. She'd be annoyed. But screw her. I'm in charge now. I wonder if the doc can be trusted. She may come in handy to me one day.*

The room fell quiet, except for the sound of two women breathing out of sync. The lights were still dimmed, and the room was blanketed in shadows as the night sky grew darker outside the windows. Carly spun round, launched at Maria again, and struck her in the chest repeatedly. Blood splattered over her face and neck, but she continued the attack until they were both red and wet. Maria's head fell back. Carly glared at the motionless psychiatrist. Her eyes were dead and blank, her chest pierced by the gold letter-opener from the office desk.

CHAPTER FIFTY

Carly walked confidently through Luton airport the following evening, her mind filled with exotic images of sun, sea and strangers. It was the longest period of time she'd held control over Grace, and the power excited her.

Once she had cleaned Maria's blood from her hands and face the previous day, Carly removed the psychiatrist's diary and Grace's notes folder from the office. She knew that inevitably her fingerprints were on the dead woman's body. But she took comfort in the fact that Grace had never been arrested, and therefore was not on the police database. Carly remembered Maria explaining she had no appointments for the next week, and with no family to check in, Carly was sure she could flee the country before the woman was found.

Unlike her first victim, unfound and wasting away deep underground, Carly wanted Maria to be discovered. It hadn't been a planned attack; the woman was simply in the wrong place at the wrong time. *The psychiatrist deserves a funeral. I'm not a total monster.*

Carly steered clear of Valerie once she returned home. She was sure Grace's mother of all people, would be able to identify the difference in personalities. She feigned a headache and locked herself in Grace's room. There she set to work in finding the passport, a small holdall for essentials and purchasing a last minute plane ticket to Alicante.

Now, stood in front of the departure board, Carly's eagerness to remain in control urged her on. She was ready to fly to Spain and begin a new life. Her own life. Deep in her thoughts, the shocking tight grip around her arm alarmed her.

"What the hell are you doing?" she screeched as she spun round.

"Grace Murphy, I am arresting you on suspicion of the murder of Maria Lee—"

"What the fuck?" Carly frustratingly twisted and turned, but she couldn't loosen Hamilton's hold on her.

"Anything you say can and will be used as evidence against you in a court of law."

"You've made a big mistake, Inspector. My name is Carly," she said.

"Tut tut. You almost got away with it, didn't you, Grace?" Hamilton replied.

"I told you, I'm not Grace."

Hamilton frowned as two uniformed policemen restrained and handcuffed Carly. They prodded her back, making her trip over her own feet before she could walk steady.

"Ms Murphy, I've met you on numerous occasions, drop the act."

"My name is Carly Murphy."

The policemen stopped, first staring at Carly and then at Hamilton.

"Don't listen to her! And don't stop walking, get her out of here now!" Hamilton ordered. "And Kerry, get her bags."

The two officers pushed Carly again and they all walked in unison.

"Got yourself a new partner, eh, Inspector?" Carly asked.

"So you do know who I am. We have met before."

"I never said we hadn't met, Detective Inspector Hamilton. I simply informed you that you had my name wrong."

The crowds watched as Carly was escorted through the airport. She glared at the two detectives walking triumphant next to her. Her eyes narrowed on the woman.

"So, a new partner?" she repeated.

"DS Fraser is part of my team. She's responsible for connecting you to Maria Lee's murder and tracking you down so quickly. I thought it would be a glorious moment for her to witness your arrest." Hamilton smirked.

"I bet you're fucking the bitch, eh, Inspector!"

Hamilton ignored her, causing Carly to roar with laughter. She didn't want to show the detectives any sign of weakness, but inside she trembled.

"You haven't denied your involvement with Maria Lee, Grace... Carly. Whatever your name is," Hamilton said.

Carly winked. "I'm saying nothing until my solicitor is present."

"The fact you feel one is necessary, makes me a happy man."

They exited the airport through the main entrance. A police car was parked directly opposite, its revolving lights flashed like a beacon to the busy holidaymakers—all slowing their pace to watch the action unfold. Carly couldn't suppress her anger any longer, she wanted answers.

"How the fuck did she know it was me?" she shouted, nodding towards Fraser.

Hamilton smiled and stepped closer. "You may have destroyed the paper trail of your appointments with Maria Lee, but you seem to have forgotten about the computer."

"What?" Carly snarled.

"Maria Lee kept a calendar of appointments on her computer, as well as all her session notes. And now that we have you in custody, I'm certain your fingerprints will match the bloody prints we found."

"That bitch shouldn't have been found for at least a week."

"If you're referring to the victim, you obviously didn't account for her book club pals turning up last night. They found the front door ajar, entered and discovered her lifeless body just hours after your appointment," Hamilton replied, his eyes glaring into hers.

Carly wanted to head-butt him, knock the patronising look from his face, but she was distracted by his new partner. The woman stood next to Hamilton, petite and pretty, gazing up to him in awe as he spoke. The rage screamed inside of Carly.

"Why did you do it Ms Murphy?" Hamilton asked.

"The doc knew too much. How did you know I would be here?" she asked.

Fraser glared at her. "The Inspector just told you—don't underestimate the power of the computer. Or the internet for that fact. It was easy to track you, when you know how."

Carly pounced forward, intent on knocking the small detective to the ground, but the two policemen who cuffed her were quicker. They pulled her back a safe distance and grappled with her. Carly couldn't take her eyes off Fraser, who had slightly stepped behind Hamilton. Her head pounded with madness, a frenzy she needed to release.

The uniformed men wrestled with her again, pushing her head down until she had no choice but to fall into the back seat of the squad car. She wanted to shriek, to shatter the glass and unleash her wrath on the woman who had halted her plans for freedom.

Outside the window, Hamilton and Fraser chatted, and she knew they were laughing at her expense. Although her hands were restrained, and resting on her back, she balled them into fists, and her body shook. The detectives turned to look at her, but Carly was only interested in making eye contact with one of them. The moment Carly locked eyes with Fraser, she glared. "I'm coming for you, Fraser." The final word leapt from her lips as the police car sped off.

EPILOGUE

"Congratulations, team! A job well done," Hamilton said as he rose his pint in the air.

"I think it's well done to Kerry," Clarke added. "You never gave up on the case, good for you." He cheered and they all clinked glasses.

A week after Grace Murphy's arrest, Hamilton felt it was time to celebrate, and invited them all to The Duke and Duchess pub across the road from the station.

"What made you flag up Maria Lee's murder, Kerry?" Morris asked after taking a sip from her wine glass.

"When the call came through to the incident room, something inside me just said I shouldn't ignore the stabbing connection."

"That's police gut instinct, that is," Wedlock shouted and knocked his pint glass against Clarke's.

Hamilton smiled. Catching suspects wasn't always an easy job, but to see the gratification it brought kept him going. "I always saw Grace Murphy as a potential victim and therefore never ran any checks on her. A lesson to be learnt there. Anyway, by the time Kerry ran a search, Grace had already purchased the plane ticket to Spain. We knew then she was doing a runner."

"But, gov," Clarke interrupted. "The whole Grace Murphy, Carly Murphy thing. Is it real? Will justice be served?"

"Look, the Met's psychiatrist evaluated her, Lewis. At the moment, it seems genuine, she has dissociative identity disorder. But she has confessed to all the murders, whether that was as Grace or Carly, who cares, right? We got what we needed. It'll be prison or a psychiatric hospital, but she's off the streets, so we did our job."

The team cheered and clinked their glasses again.

"I just find it nuts that another personality can take over your body and control you," Clarke continued.

"But can we truly believe that?" Morris argued. "Look at the victims, they were all important to Grace. They were victims of her revenge. Women she went to school or socialised with, a colleague and the nurse at her grandfather's hospice, and of course her psychiatrist. Does she really expect us to believe her story that someone else took over her body and she had no idea?"

Wedlock puffed his cheeks and exhaled deeply. "This is too heavy for a night at The Duke when the boss is paying. Whatever her story, we caught her. We never have to see her again. So drink up and same again please." He winked in Hamilton's direction.

Hamilton laughed. It was always good to have a joker on the team. The three continued their debate while he walked to the bar, happy to buy his team another round. Fraser stood next to him and fumbled with a beer mat.

"You should look happier than that, Kerry." He nudged her arm.

"Oh, I'm happy, sir," she hesitated. "There's just one thing playing on my mind."

"Pray tell." He smiled.

"Grace, or Carly, or whoever… she said she was coming for me."

Hamilton rested his hand on her slender shoulder. "Never worry about what a suspect says when they're arrested. It's all in the heat of the moment, their anger at being caught. She can't lay a finger on you."

THE END

A NOTE FROM BLOODHOUND BOOKS

Thanks for reading In The Shadows. We hope you enjoyed it as much as we did. Please consider leaving a review on Amazon or Goodreads to help others find and enjoy this book too.

We make every effort to ensure that books are carefully edited and proofread, however occasionally mistakes do slip through. If you spot something, please do send details to info@bloodhoundbooks.com and we can amend it.

Bloodhound Books specialise in crime and thriller fiction. We regularly have special offers including free and discounted eBooks. To be the first to hear about these special offers, why not join our mailing list here? We won't send you more than two emails per month and we'll never pass your details on to anybody else.

Readers who enjoyed In The Shadows will also enjoy the next two books in the DI Hamilton series by Tara Lyons

No Safe Home

Deadly Friendship

Lightning Source UK Ltd.
Milton Keynes UK
UKHW041244240820
368744UK00003B/214